GHOST HUNTERS

BONES IN THE WALL

SUSAN MCCAULEY

Publisher: Celtic Sea Publishing, 13165 W Lake Houston Pkwy, Houston, TX 77044

Cover copyright Christian Bentulan.

ISBN: 978-1-951069-04-9

Formatted by Dragon Realm Press
www.dragonrealmpress.com

For my Alex, be happy and always follow your heart.

CONTENTS

CHAPTER ONE

Morning mist clung to the ghostball field like spiderwebs. I shifted from one foot to the other, waiting for the ghostball to appear. I caught a quick glimpse as it streaked past; the swirling symbols on the ball that trapped the poltergeist inside flared gold. The ball dodged right, then left. I dashed after it, barely aware of Mom and half my school screaming my name from the sidelines. If I made this goal, my team would win the play-offs and we'd be headed to the state championship!

It was now or never.

I ran straight for the jittering ghostball. And kicked it with all my strength.

The poltergeist energy that powered the ball didn't stand a chance. I grinned as the ghostball soared through the air and straight into the goal at the opposite end of the field.

Cheers erupted from the sidelines, and before I could catch my breath, my best friend and teammate, Jason, had shot off the bench and into the middle of the players. He helped hoist me above their heads. I'd done it, and we'd won the play-off game! Next week we'd head for the Louisiana State Ghostball Championship!

I whooped and pumped my fist into the air. I was the first ever sixth grader at Rey Middle to score the final point to take us to a championship game.

Our team captain, Tommy Lord, and my other teammates surrounded me. "Alex. Alex. Alex." They chanted like wild banshees set loose on a battlefield.

"You were awesome, X!" Jason grabbed me and gave me a half-hug, half–back slap. I laughed and yanked on his ghostball shirt, glad he was part of the team and our victory. The only reason he was even on the team was because of me. He secretly hated ghostball. Unless he was watching his home team, the Jamaican Nationals. My grin was so big I felt like my face would split in two.

"Great job, champ!" Mom plopped a quick kiss on my head before I could stop her. Oh, well, one kiss wouldn't hurt my rep too much, and we'd won! Nothing could be better than that. Mom put her arm around me and gave me a squeeze. "I'm so proud of you."

"Thanks." Still smiling, I looked around and my heart dropped. "Where's Dad?"

Mom's smile wavered, but she forced it to stay in place. "He had an unexpected showing for a client. But don't worry. He'll be there at the championship game."

Right. It was like Dad to miss the important stuff. And for what? Some stupid real estate sale. I shoved away the twinge in my chest and focused on the people still chanting my name. On the people that really mattered. I forced all my cheerfulness into my voice and hugged Mom and Jason back. "Well, I'm glad you're here."

A week later and it was time for the championship game . . . but first, I had to renew the protection against ghosts in my room. The wards—protective symbols to stop them from getting inside. If I didn't renew my wards, Mom would never let me hear the end of it. Just imagine if a ghost got into the house while we were away at the game. She'd never let me play again! Then my life would be over.

I added a dab of white paint to the pentacle on my bedroom window, making sure each of the five points of the star were enclosed by a circle, and then hung a Seal of Solomon from a nail in the wall. Perfect. No ghosts would get through that. We had to use magical symbols, called sigils, to ward against ghosts. If we didn't, they'd get inside and wreak total havoc.

I pulled on my team jersey, grabbed my warded cleats and game bag, and headed for the car.

Mom was already waiting, keys in hand. "Ready for the big game, champ?"

"Definitely." I hurled my bag and myself into the backseat. What an awesome way to end my sixth-grade year.

"And your wards and sigils have been renewed?" Mom adjusted the rearview mirror and then checked the Third Pentacle of Jupiter she had painted on the interior roof of our station wagon along with every other protective psychic symbol she knew how to paint; never mind that Seals of Solomon and wards against spirits were also etched in the glass of every car window as soon as it rolled off the production line. As an occult historian, she was ultra-paranoid.

"Mom." I rolled my eyes and scratched at the sigil at the base of my skull, a miniature black Third Pentacle of Jupiter that was tattooed on every child as soon as it was born and blessed. Mine always itches when I'm nervous. When I was younger my parents worried that I might be one of the 4 percent of the population who is actually psychic, and that I'd be apprenticed to some psychic far away so I could learn to protect the Untouched. The Untouched. Those are the people who can't hear or see ghosts. Thankfully, that didn't happen. I'm as Untouched as you can get. "There were no breaches in my room or my cleats. All of my sigils are fine."

She glanced in the rearview mirror again. "I still don't understand why you have to play ghostball. Maybe you can try soccer next year?"

"Mom—" I flopped myself against the backseat and clicked on my seat belt. "Soccer is so boring. Ghostball is fun. We have to kick the ball everywhere we want it to go in soccer. With ghostball you never know where it'll go on its own." But that wasn't what was nagging her. What she really wanted to know was why I'd play a game where a sigil could get damaged, letting a poltergeist loose. She bugged me about that at least sixteen hundred times a week, which is nuts, because if that ever did happen—a huge IF—then the team psychic would handle it.

"I just don't like the game . . ." she muttered. Translation: I won. It was such a silly thing to worry about and she knew it. Poltergeists were supposed to be really nasty, but they'd never been alive. It's not like we were playing with people's souls. She pushed the remote and the garage door creaked open, revealing a gray sky. "Dad has to show a house this morning, but he'll try to meet us at the game."

I dug my fingernails into my hand, leaving little crescent-shaped marks. Yeah, right. Typical Dad.

We drove in silence watching the usual morning fog clear from the twisted Mississippi River. She merged onto the main roadway and gasped.

In the rearview mirror, I saw her eyes widen.

She slammed on the brakes. Our car swerved, jerking the seat belt hard across my chest. Metal screeched. A horn blared. Glass smashed and flew everywhere. My heart launched itself into my throat and strangled my cry.

Sound and motion melded together.

The side of the car crunched down on my hip and searing pain screamed down my leg. Then everything went black.

A rhythmic beeping was the first thing I heard. The throbbing in my leg pounded like a jackhammer. I tried to move my toes, but couldn't. My eyes were crusted closed, but I didn't want to open them anyway. Everything hurt. My body was broken.

Someone squeezed my hand. Okay, maybe that didn't hurt. I pried my eyes open and looked up. "Mom?" I croaked.

Mom was there holding my hand, worried but uninjured. "I'm here."

My leg was in a cast and hanging from some strap-like thing attached to the hospital bed. A jumble of tubes and wires ran to and from my body. Tears spilled down my cheeks. "I'll never play ghostball again."

That was all I could say. Fear and anger battled inside me. How could this have happened? Why?

But Mom just squeezed my hand harder, and instead of the everything's-going-to-be-all-right smile she usually gave me when I was hurt, there was only sadness. "You're alive. And you will heal. That's what matters."

Mom slipped something cool and smooth into my palm. Her Nazar Boncuğu amulet—a bright blue-and-white glass eye that protects the wearer from evil. She got it at a conference of occult scholars in Turkey, and hadn't removed it since. "You need this more than I do."

"Why? There are plenty of hospital sigils."

Her neck, usually decorated with the brilliant blue eye, now looked pale and vulnerable. Mom glanced toward the door, which was wide open, then back at me. "I have to go. But remember, I love you." With one last squeeze of my fingers, she stood and walked out the door.

My heart sped up and battled its way into my throat. Why would she be leaving me here? Alone? Like this? And why in Solomon's name had she given me her amulet? A wave of pain crashed over me and I settled back against the stiff hospital bed, inhaling the sickening scent of antiseptic.

I looked from my casted leg to the tubes in my arm, to the window. Large, strange symbols were etched there. Psychics' symbols. Far more complicated than any seals I knew how to draw. Hospitals took ghosts seriously, especially here in New Orleans—the most haunted city in America. They had to. If one crazy ghost broke through an old ward or damaged sigil, a dozen or more lives would be snuffed out—and that was if the federal psychics arrived in time. I glanced at the small alcove I'd grown so accustomed to in my gram's hospital room before she passed: the prayer station, complete with a Bible, Torah, Koran, and an iron ghost trap etched with several Seals of Solomon.

If someone died and didn't want to cross over, the hospital psychics would be ready, no matter which religion the ghost had practiced. But only if the spirit lingered. Most cross over. It's when they don't that the trouble starts and the feds are called in. I shivered.

"Who left this open?" A nurse came in, made a tutting sound, and closed the warded door to my room.

Seeing I was awake she scurried to my bedside and checked the beeping machine. "You're very lucky to be alive. Your father will be so glad to see you awake."

She walked out of the room with no further explanation. I didn't know how long I'd been unconscious. Days? Weeks? Maybe Mom left because she needed a break and Dad was taking over. That made sense.

I slipped Mom's amulet around my neck and tucked it beneath my hospital gown so I wouldn't lose it.

A few minutes later, Dad came in, his eyes swollen and puffy and red.

"It's okay, Dad." I forced my words through a parched throat. "I'm okay." I looked at my mangled leg and cringed. "Well, sort of."

He sat next to me and took up my hand. The same hand Mom had just let go of.

"Did Mom go home to get some rest? She looked tired."

Dad swallowed hard. "She . . ." His voice cracked. "She didn't make it."

"Didn't make what? She was just here."

Dad stroked a strand of hair from my face. "She died, Alex."

A sick, sinking sensation writhed in my stomach. That was impossible. It had to be. "She was just here." I held up my hand, entwined with Dad's. "Holding this hand."

He squeezed my fingers harder. "She died in the car accident, son. Three days ago."

My world blurred with tears. She couldn't be dead. She'd just been here, holding my hand.

Hadn't she?

Chapter Two·

Nothing had changed. Same river. Same swamps. Same fog. Same gray sky. Except somehow summer had passed me by in a drug-induced haze while I recovered from the surgeries that had put my shattered hip back together. Now I was home to face my shattered life.

The last winds of summer rustled through the treetops, the leaves dancing in the morning light. We passed the Garden District Psychic Office, the one people in our neighborhood called when the federal psychics were backlogged or didn't respond. We finally passed Lafayette Cemetery No. 1 where Mom was buried—intricate sigils burned and twisted into the wrought iron of its massive gates. There were no new graves at Lafayette, but Dad's great-grandparents had a family tomb there for us to use. Just what I'd always wanted—to be buried in a city of the dead. Not.

I shivered and looked away from the haunting gates. I was the only one in the family who hadn't visited Mom's grave. Dad had. Aunt Trudy had. Aunt Elena had. Even my weird cousin Hannah had. Dad said I shouldn't feel guilty, and that I needed to focus on healing. Well, I'd had three months to heal, yet I was still in constant pain. I still felt utterly broken inside.

Dad turned his car down our cobbled street and pulled up to the garage. We sat in the driveway for a few minutes not saying anything. What could we say? Home was here, but Mom was gone and my old life was over.

"Looks like they repainted the wards." Dad's voice cracked.

I looked at the glowing Arabic and Hebrew Seals of Solomon that covered our garage door. He was right. The paint was fresh. The city's

Office of Psychic Intervention, or OPI as most of us called it, repainted exterior doors every three months to decrease the likelihood of spirit attacks. If only the spiritualists back in 1900 hadn't opened the door to the other side that no one could close, then we wouldn't have to worry about ghosts and the whole world would have stayed normal. We'd had more than one hundred years to heal, and still most of the Untouched considered psychics little better than criminals for that one unforgivable sin. That first outpouring of spirits had cost people their lives. Now the psychics were a necessary evil, a dry, brittle hedge against a second scourge. Dad said they were like the IRS, only worse. Whatever that meant.

I glanced back at the sigils on our house. They'd been repainted the week before Mom and I had left for the ghostball championship. I hated ghostball. If I hadn't been in that stupid championship game, the accident would never have happened. Mom would still be alive.

Dad carried my small suitcase into the house, leaving me to trail behind him. The front room looked exactly as I remembered it. Except darker. And cold. Maybe autumn would arrive early this year.

He lit the furnace, which came to life with a rumbling moan. The curtains were drawn and I ran my finger along the dusty side table, stopping before I touched Mom's reading glasses. The last book she'd been reading lay there, still marked at the halfway point. "It looks like no one's lived here for months."

"No one has." Dad's voice was cold, dead. "I've spent nearly every night at the hospital with you. Now that your aunts and Hannah live next door, they've checked in on the place when I was at the hospital—picked up the mail, watered the plants, checked the sigils, renewed the wards, but I told them not to move anything."

"Why'd they come here, anyway?" I snapped, wishing they'd stayed in Boston. "It's not like you were ever really close." I didn't want anyone intruding on me—trying to "help" me get over the accident when it wasn't something I was going to get over.

Dad scowled, but ignored my tone. "Trudy and Hannah've had a hard time since your uncle David left them, which is why Elena moved in with them. Besides, Elena needed to save money to grow her—business, which should thrive here." He shrugged. "Anyway, living near each other seemed like a good idea."

"Really? Crazy Aunt Elena? She's living next door?" Dad had told me that Aunt Trudy and my cousin Hannah moved from Boston to help him when Mom died, but had failed to mention Aunt Elena. I couldn't imagine Dad had planned on having his wannabe psychic sister living so close.

Mom had been an academic. She'd studied the history of everything that had happened in the psychic realm. But Aunt Elena. Aunt Elena was the black sheep of our entire family; she had embraced the psychics and the supernatural. We barely ever saw her and now she was our neighbor. I wondered what Mom would think.

I tried to ignore the gnawing pain that Mom was gone when I half expected her to burst through the kitchen door with a batch of chocolate chip cookies. I wouldn't have wanted to stay here alone either. Maybe having them close would help Dad. Maybe.

"Things'll be fine, Alex. You'll see." Dad forced a smile onto his tired face and batted at his favorite throw pillow, sending a cloud of dust into the air. He coughed. "Needs a bit of tidying up, is all."

I swallowed and limped forward, the ache in my leg a constant companion. "I just want to go to my room."

"I understand." He gripped my suitcase hard and led me up the stairs, one painful step at a time.

My door was closed, the colorful sigils Mom had painted last spring still vivid. She was gone, but lingered everywhere.

Dad set my bag down inside the door to my room, and I sat on my bed. We stared at each other.

"Let me know if you need anything?" Dad looked at me, then the room. "And check your sigils. They haven't been renewed in months."

Right. Just what I wanted to do first thing back home. "I will."

He nodded and backed out the door, closing it behind him.

The sigils on my bedroom windows looked solid enough. They could wait. What I needed was a nap. I lay back on the covers and let the softness of my own pillows, my own bed, my own room wrap around me. But there was a huge hole in my chest that wouldn't let me enjoy it. No matter how much I'd missed home, I missed Mom more.

I rolled onto my side facing my nightstand and looked at the picture I kept there. One of me and Mom and Dad at the least haunted beach in America last summer. What a fantastic trip. No extra wards to worry about. Sun. Sand. Fun.

I grabbed an extra pillow and hugged it tightly, refusing to acknowledge the tears that streamed down my cheeks. It seemed like I lay there for hours before I finally fell asleep.

A cool breeze wafted across my face and ruffled my hair. "Alex . . . Oh, Alex." The woman's voice was soft, hollow. At first I thought it might be Mom. But then I remembered: Mom's dead.

I peeked from beneath the covers. The curtains in my bedroom window fluttered in the moonlight. But there was no breeze. The window was closed. A cold sense of dread gnawed at my gut. I'd forgotten to check the sigils.

Closing my eyes tight, I prayed no ghosts had gotten inside.

"Alex." She was closer. Right over the bed. Right next to my ear. "I'm so excited to finally get a chance to talk to you after all these years."

Years? Cold seeped into the covers, and I shivered. I felt her staring at me.

"Sit up and talk to me, child. I'm so glad you're home. You gave your father a scare," she prattled on. "I know you're awake."

This wasn't happening. I wasn't a psychic and there's no way I could hear or see ghosts. It had to be some sort of trauma-induced psychosis like Dr. Midgley had talked about before I left the hospital.

"Alex." Her voice punched through my feathery pillow with a cold blast.

Oh. My. Gosh. No way. She can't be real.

"I know you can hear me," she cooed. "Come, now, talk to Mrs. Wilson." She reached over to pat my arm, but her hand passed right through me, leaving a chilly slug-like trail on my skin.

I clenched my teeth and tried not to scream. Could someone feel a hallucination?

"Oh, goodness. You must still be tired. How silly of me." I felt her float past my bed toward the window. "It's the middle of the night and tomorrow's your first day back at Rey, isn't it? They released you in time for a new school year."

The lump of fear thickened in my throat. How'd she know I went to Henry Louis Rey Middle School? She must've been living—er, residing— in our house without us knowing. I shivered to think of what she knew about us, then laughed at myself. Nonsense. It was all in my head. Only Class A and B Psychics could hear and see ghosts. I wasn't even a Class C. I had no psychic abilities.

"You know, I attended middle school here back in . . . let's see . . ." I could almost see her counting back the years. "Must've been, oh, sixty years ago now. Lots of changes since then." She clicked her tongue. "Lots of changes."

I shut my eyes so hard that tears squeezed out. What was I supposed to do? Talk to her? Ignore her? Maybe if I ignored her, she'd stop talking. And if she stopped talking, then I'd know she wasn't real.

"Well, if you're going to be rude and ignore me, I suppose I'd better head back to the living room," she huffed.

If she wasn't real, I wouldn't be able to see her. I peeked between a gap in my pillows and swallowed my gasp. Not two feet away floated a translucent tub of a woman, moving away from me through a box of old ghostball trophies.

"Perhaps your father is watching something good tonight. That man . . . he usually only keeps on those crime shows." She floated into the whitewashed wall, her voice muted, and then faded altogether when she disappeared.

I leapt from my bed and rummaged around my drawer of ward supplies. Maybe I was going crazy, but just in case I wasn't, I needed protection. So there I stood at two o'clock in the morning in my underwear repainting every ward in my bedroom. It took hours before I finally drifted back to sleep.

The windup alarm clock rang, dancing across my bedside table. I smashed the obnoxious thing to silence it. Mom and Dad wouldn't allow us to have electric clocks. Mom said there was too much chance of a ghost getting through the electrical currents, and that having a TV was bad enough. I saw the ward supplies on my nightstand and almost laughed. I must have had a nightmare. That made sense; it was my first night home after all that had happened. My first night home without Mom.

I shivered. I should have died in that accident. Not Mom. I clenched my teeth, not sure which nightmare was worse—the one I had when sleeping, or the one I was living while awake. I forced myself to think of something else entirely.

Throwing back the covers, I limped over to my dresser, pulled a pair of clean boxers over the still-red scar that curved from my left butt cheek down to my thigh, tossed on an old ghostball T-shirt, and shimmied into a pair of jeans.

Why did I have to go back to school today? Ugh. Dad would have let me stay home for a few weeks if Dr. Midgley hadn't insisted that a "return to normalcy" was the best thing for me.

"Alex?" Dad called up the stairs. "Ready to go, champ?"

No. I wasn't ready. I'd never be ready again. If it were up to me I'd have stayed in the hospital indefinitely. I didn't want to be home, and I didn't want to go to school. I'd managed to push off visits from my ghostball teammates, but now I wouldn't have a choice. I'd have to talk to them, even though all I wanted was to be left alone.

I slung my backpack over my shoulder and shuffled down the stairs.

Fresh squeezed OJ and a bowl of granola waited for me on the table. Dad took a bite out of a bagel. "I'll bet your team can't wait to see you. You know Jason called at least seven times yesterday. He's so excited you're finally home."

He probably was excited. Jason and I had spent nearly every day of our lives together since we were five. I missed him, too. But what if I wasn't the same Alex as before?

"Jason wanted to come over and visit, but I told him you'd be back to school today. It'll be great." Dad bit a large chunk out of his cream cheese–slathered bagel. "Back to normal."

"Yeah, great." I tried to fake a smile, but I could barely force one onto my face.

"School's only been in session for a week. You'll be fine." Dad popped the last bite of bagel into his mouth and picked up his briefcase. "I've got to show a house in fifteen minutes, but I'll be home early so we can pick up the place a bit. Maybe watch a movie?"

"Sure." I shrugged, but I really wanted to crawl into my bed and never get out.

"Oh, and I talked to my sister today. She's having a birthday party for Hannah on Saturday."

"A what?" I stopped eating and pushed the bowl of granola away from me with disgust. I'd stopped having birthday parties at ten, like most kids. After we turned ten and went through our psychic testing to determine if we were psychic, there were no more birthday parties.

"She's new at Rey and doesn't have any friends yet. I thought it'd be good for you both. She'll help you get back into the swing of things, and you can introduce her to your friends."

I studied Dad and took a sip of orange juice. Could he actually be serious? Truly? Hannah was weird. An outcast. She always did her own thing, no matter if she looked like a freak. There was no way I was going to introduce her to anyone I knew.

Dad tried on his most winning smile. "I said we'd go."

Orange juice almost sprayed out of my nose, but I sniffed it back in one burning snort-swallow. "No way. I'm not going."

"Alex." Dad set his briefcase down and sat beside me. "You pushed away your teammates while you were in the hospital."

"Not Jason," I growled. "I let him visit me."

Dad held up his hands. "Jason's different, I know . . . but you can't push away family. And they moved here for us. Besides, the doctors think it's best for you to get back to your normal routine as soon as possible. I thought a party and time with family might help you get back to your old self." Dad tussled my unbrushed mop of blond hair. Who knows the last time I had a haircut; probably when Mom took me.

My old self? I would never be my old self again. I scowled and crossed my arms over my chest.

"I miss your mother, too. Always will. But we have to keep moving forward." Dad squared his shoulders. "It's what she'd want."

Anger flooded my chest. Was he kidding? I'd just gotten home and he wanted me to forget about Mom and go to my bizarre-o cousin's birthday party? Not happening. He may have heaved off the weight of Mom's death in the past three months, but I hadn't. I never would.

I shouldn't even be alive. I should be dead—just like Mom. I didn't have time for friends, new or old. I was too busy trying to heal my leg. Too busy trying to deal with a life without Mom. Too busy trying to figure out if the woman I'd seen in my bedroom last night was real or in my head. Because if I was seeing dead people, there was a lot more wrong with me than a busted hip.

CHAPTER THREE

I arrived at school early, Mom's amulet tucked beneath my T-shirt, and hoped I'd be spared from my teammates' concerned looks and high fives to each other about the first ghostball victory of the season. Seventh grade had just started, but I already felt left behind.

The halls were almost like a ghost town this early, so I shuffled my way to give my "Alex Lenard is able to return to work/school" paperwork to the seventh-grade secretary, then slowly headed to my new locker to enhance my sigils. Of course, all our lockers came with prefabricated sigils etched into the metal, but students were encouraged to add their own both for extra protection and so they wouldn't forget what they'd learned in elementary sigil classes.

One by one the kids filled up the hallway. A few glanced at me, others stared. My teammates rushed over to me.

"Hey, Alex. Welcome back." Ethan Quake, a teammate, slapped my back. "Hope you can come back soon. It's not the same without you."

My stomach churned and sweat broke out on my forehead. I shut my eyes and took a few calming breaths. "Thanks," I mumbled. "I'm not sure if the doctors will let me play for a while."

"Well, that's okay. You should still come to practice to keep yourself sharp."

I nodded, but had no intention of sitting in on practice. The last place I wanted to be was near a ghostball game.

Tommy bumped my fist and then headed off to class.

A few of the other guys gave me awkward high fives and then went their separate ways. Oh, this was going to be a long day.

The tardy bell rang as I collapsed into my desk for last period. Occult History. Basically, a historical overview about King Solomon and how angels had visited him and given him the knowledge to create the seals we used today. Jewish. Muslim. Christian. King Solomon was in all of the major religious books and we all used his seals.

I was not in the mood for a review of everything we'd already learned in elementary school. Oh, well, at least I'd come back to school on a Friday; I'd have all weekend to recover from the stares and whispers floating around me like gnats. I was no longer the school ghostball champion. Now I was Alex, the kid whose mom got killed in that car accident. The kid with a limp. At least they couldn't see the scars.

"Buck up, man." My best friend, Jason Anderson, grinned at me over his Occult History journal. Thankfully some things hadn't changed.

Even though Jason was the opposite of everything I had been, he was always there for me. I was white. He was black. My hair stood on end. His hair was short and tidy. I was good at school and good with friends. Jason tolerated school and had one friend: me. Yep. Best friends— ever since first grade when he arrived from Jamaica and no one else would sit with him at lunch. They thought his accent was weird. I thought it was cool. And his mom always made sure we had the best macaroni and cheese on the planet. That was her specialty. Jason loved to eat and he liked to hunt. I didn't hunt. I liked sports. He coped with them. He'd even joined the school ghostball team because I was on it. I suppose that was the biggest thing we had in common: loyalty. We always had each other's backs. No matter what.

Jason hunched low and whispered, "Hey. You gotta come over for dinner next week. Mom's planning to make a huge batch of mac 'n' cheese just for you. Your dad wouldn't let her bring any into the hospital because you couldn't eat much and he said he'd end up eating it all and would get fat." He chuckled softly, his gleaming smile infectious. "And she said we can play as many video games as we want. You know my mom. If you don't come she'll whup your backside."

He winked and I couldn't help but feel better. Even if I had changed, Jason was still Jason. And he was more than a friend. He was family.

"So is Grimes making you give your start-of-year presentation?" he asked, his mischievous brown eyes sparkling.

I shook my head no. Thankfully she'd taken pity on me and let me miss this assignment.

"For those of you who didn't have the opportunity to give your presentation yesterday, you'll have a chance today." Ms. Grimes, our cool, punk-like Occult History teacher with maroon-streaked hair, picked up a clipboard and checked to see who still needed to present.

I slumped down in my chair, thankful to be seated in the back row, and leaned my head against the wall for a nap. Hopefully Ms. Grimes wouldn't notice. And if she did, Jason would cover for me.

Several kids droned on about their summer breaks and how their mothers had made them wear T-shirts with sigils on them for extra protection over the summer break.

I'm not sure why parents still spent money on sigiled shirts. My mom had lectured on their ineffectiveness at conferences. Besides, the Third Pentacle of Jupiter tattoos we were all given at birth were nearly impenetrable—most of the time. Since the Great Unleashing in 1900, when a group of British and American spiritualists tore a hole between our world and the spirit world allowing spirits in, people took their precautions seriously, but still. Overkill much?

The Great Unleashing didn't stop the scientists and inventors. They'd kept working with electricity, even when they found out spirits used the electrical currents to travel. That's when the psychics became important to society. They were still blamed for letting spirits loose on us, but now people needed them to help control the ghosts.

Most of us weren't psychics, and the Untouched just wanted to live our lives with as little paranormal interaction as possible. Now and then a kid who wanted to tick off his parents would rebel and wipe a sigil off his bedroom window. But most kids wouldn't dare. There'd been enough cases of hauntings to scare us away from doing that—even with our wards. I soon lost track of my thoughts, my mind blipping in and out of sleep.

"My aunt gave this to me for my birthday. It's a Deluxe Ghost Hunting Kit." My cousin Hannah's voice shattered my slumber. Oh, dear Lord, I had no idea she would be in any of my classes.

There she stood, all in black, with thick, round glasses that made it look like her eyes were bugging out of her head. She looked like a Pretender if I'd ever seen one.

Several girls giggled, but my eyes shot open and I leaned forward. Wait. Did she say Deluxe Ghost Hunting Kit? Was my cousin actually a Pretender?

Pretenders pretended to be psychic and their false claims had led to spirit-related injuries. Which made them as welcome as you'd expect. Paranormal investigators were okay—they did some good, even if they weren't psychic.

Last time I saw her—granted it was before her father left two years ago—she couldn't have cared less about the supernatural. I even remember Aunt Trudy getting mad at her for getting a C in warding class. Now she wore head-to-toe black, her dirt-brown hair with bangs that hung below her eyebrows. She opened a large, gunmetal-gray hardcover case. "It's everything a serious paranormal investigator needs."

If she heard the snickers echoing around the room, she didn't seem to notice or care. Typical Hannah. She never cared what anyone thought of her. "It has a Gauss Master EMF meter. EMF stands for electromagnetic field. It lets you know if there are shifts in the electromagnetic field caused by electrically charged objects or entities. It also has a portable motion sensor to detect movement by unseen forms."

"Woooooooo," howled a burly boy called Billy at the front of the class. Everyone burst out laughing. Everyone except for Hannah and me and the teacher.

"That's enough," Ms. Grimes snapped. The class reluctantly settled down under her icy gaze. "I'm sorry, Hannah. Please continue."

Hannah bobbed her head, a determined look in her eye. "Just because we're Untouched doesn't mean we can't understand more about the paranormal. We can't leave all the work for the psychics. If it wasn't for local paranormal investigators, we'd have spirits running amok all over town."

The class shifted uncomfortably, obviously not wanting to think about lurking spirits. No one did, even if it was part of our lives. It was a part we'd rather ignore until we had a problem. But Hannah pushed on, her eyes appearing nearly as big as the frames of her owl-like glasses. "The OPI is backlogged. And the town psychics can only do so much. That's where paranormal investigators come in." She lifted another gadget. "This is an EVP listener. EVP stands for electronic voice phenomena. There are some really cool EVPs different paranormal investigators have captured." She pointed to some sort of temperature gauge. "And this is a digital local remote thermometer to check for dips in air temperature, which can sometimes indicate the presence of an entity."

"That's, ah, very interesting, Hannah." Ms. Grimes sat on the edge of her desk, her hands twitching in her lap. "But isn't it best to leave the paranormal investigations for trained psychics?"

Hannah patted the lid of her kit. "Of course we need psychics, but so many people are afraid of them or angry at them because they started the Problem. But paranormal investigators are normal people like you and me."

Ms. Grimes put her hand to her heart like the thought of her becoming a paranormal investigator might make it stop beating.

"We can be an integral part of the ward system if given a chance. Paranormal investigators can be a town's first line of defense—especially if the federal and town psychics are busy. There've even been cases where PIs have helped spirits cross over." She grinned, excitement coloring her pale cheeks, her eyes darting around the room. "Trained paranormal investigators can help filter out the smaller cases from the bigger ones, giving more time for the government psychics to actually do their jobs. There is a place in the ghost-hunting arena for Untouched. We just need the proper training."

Ghost hunters were freakish, and ghosts—well, they were plain scary. I'd lived my life surrounded by wards and sigils and no ghosts whatsoever, which was fine by me. And most of the population.

Ms. Grimes took a deep breath. "I see . . . Is there anything else?"

Hannah scanned the class. "Are there any questions?"

Jason raised his hand and I nearly slid under my desk. Was he trying to embarrass me?

Hannah reluctantly nodded to him.

"So, what type of phenomena have you actually captured with that stuff?" Jason asked.

"Nothing."

A few kids looked at each other and rolled their eyes.

Hannah frowned. "I just received the kit. So I haven't had a chance to capture anything—yet. But I'm going with my aunt on an investigation this weekend and—"

"And, what?" sneered David, a boy with spiky brown hair. "You gonna capture a ghost in a bottle and bring it in for show-and-tell?"

Everyone laughed and Hannah's cheeks grew pink.

"That's quite enough, David. I'm sure Hannah will keep us posted if she finds anything." In small movements, Ms. Grimes renewed the ward on her desk. "Thank you, Hannah."

Hannah closed the case among barely veiled snickers. Most Untouched wouldn't be caught anywhere near paranormal equipment. Sure we used wards and sigils like sunscreen, but we didn't want to invite the paranormal into our lives any more than it already was. Most Untouched hate psychics. We simply accepted them as a part of life.

I couldn't believe my two aunts and cousin now lived next door to me. And that my cousin was in my Occult History class. Why in Solomon's name did Hannah have to be into that stuff? Being a psychic—or even a Pretender—was like being the smartest kid in school with bad breath and body odor. You steered clear of them. If my old teammates found out she was my cousin, I'd never hear the end of it. Jason would make fun of me, but I could deal with him.

It wasn't long after Hannah's presentation that the final bell rang. Jason took off fast, reminding me about his doctor appointment after snickering about my cousin's presentation.

I tossed my books into my backpack and bolted through a throng of kids toward my locker, trying to avoid Hannah. I hit a wet patch and limp-skidded straight into the door with a metallic bang.

A couple eighth-grader jocks laughed, but I tried to ignore them. I slowed down, stood up tall, and focused on my combination, not letting them see my tears.

Before I fumbled through my new locker combination and dumped my books, someone tapped me on the shoulder.

"Hey, Alex," a girl's voice squeaked. Hannah.

"Hey." I forced a smile. "I didn't know you'd be in one of my classes."

"Cool, isn't it?" She tried to smile, but failed. She stared at me with red-rimmed eyes that said she'd been crying. "At least I know one person here."

A surge of guilt swept through me. I never thought that she might actually feel lonely here. Maybe she hadn't even wanted to leave her old friends or school or home in the first place.

"Hey, Lenard." My old ghostball captain, Tommy Lord, walked up and looked from me to Hannah. "Making new friends?"

I opened my locker, tossed in a book, grabbed the ones I'd need for the weekend, and slammed the door shut. "No."

Hannah stuck out her hand, which Tommy shook like a wet fish. "Actually, I'm Alex's cousin, Hannah Stevenson."

Why can't I be invisible?

Tommy's eyes widened at me. "Your cousin? Wow." Tommy let her hand drop and Hannah bolted down the hall—away from the awkwardness.

Great. Not only did she dress like a freak show, but news about her paranormal interests must already be spreading. That's just what I needed on top of everything else.

"I know you've been out of the game for three months and all, but we need you back. You and Jason both. It's not the same without you." Tommy frowned and gave a little shake of his head that made his sandy brown bangs fall into his eyes.

"Jason quit?" I asked.

"You didn't know?"

I shook my head. I hadn't wanted to talk about ghostball, not even to Jason.

"You're our best player and with you out and Jason gone, it's been—hard. So, I'm hoping if you get back to it, he will, too. We need to rebuild our team. What do you say?"

No pressure. "Umm . . . I can't play, Tommy." I gestured to my leg. "It was pretty bad. I can't play for a while."

"Well, you can still come to practice so you're ready to get back to it soon as you're healed."

"Maybe." There was no way I was going to play ghostball again, but I didn't want to get into that right now. Jason might go back, but I doubted he'd rejoin if I didn't. I hoisted my backpack over my shoulder, turned toward the bus, and stopped dead.

An elderly, dark-skinned janitor stood in front of me, a man I'd never seen before. His gleaming smile was overshadowed by the five oozing bullet holes in his translucent body. Two in his face, three in his chest.

Dark blood still seeped from them. "Don't you let anyone pressure you, son. You'll adjust to your new situation soon enough."

The tingle of dread I'd felt in my bedroom spread through my gut, and my breath caught.

"You all right there?" the kind, croaky voice asked.

Shivers slithered over my skin and my heart slammed against my ribs like a bird trying to escape its cage.

A hand landed with a thud on my shoulder, jolting me with terror. Tommy Lord looked down at me. "Just think about it, okay, Lenard?" Tommy was totally unaware of the bloody apparition not four feet from us.

My gaze flickered nervously from Tommy's face to the dead man. Chills spilled down my spine. Two ghosts in one day. It's not possible. If you're not psychic by age ten, you're never psychic. So they can't be real. I can't be psychic. I'm having hallucinations or something.

"I'll think about it," I mumbled and tore away from Tommy, hobbling as fast as I could to the bus. Three months ago, I'd have done anything for Tommy Lord and our ghostball team. Now, he'd think I was some sort of freak who was too scared to talk. But there was no way I was up to facing a shot-up ghost, if he was even real.

I spared one final glance backward. The bullet-holed janitor stood there leaning on his ghost mop, smiling.

Susan McCauley

CHAPTER FOUR

I slid into my usual chair at the breakfast table and inhaled a deep whiff of warm pancakes and maple syrup. This was the first Saturday morning home since the accident. No more hospital food. Dad made pancakes, and Jason had come over wearing his pajamas, just like he had almost every Saturday before this living nightmare. I remembered when we were younger and we'd both worn footy pajamas for Saturday morning breakfast; his had been green with dancing monkeys. I almost laughed, but couldn't. Mom wasn't here and I was still seeing ghosts. First Mrs. Wilson, then the janitor. Or were they hallucinations? If only Mom were here, I'd tell her everything and she'd know what to do. But she wasn't, and I couldn't tell Dad or his sisters.

Real or not, Mrs. Wilson hovered a few feet away, floating lazily along the ceiling humming to herself. Dad and Jason hadn't even glanced her direction. She had to be in my head—I'm twelve, and nobody becomes psychic when they're this old. Ever.

"So, how was the first day back?" Dad asked and chomped down on a piece of crispy bacon, looking from me to Jason.

Jason took a huge bite from his triple stack of pancakes, gave Dad a thumbs-up, and talked with his mouth full. "He did great, Mr. Lenard."

"I survived." I licked a dollop of syrup from the corner of my mouth, not meeting Dad's eyes.

Dad set his coffee cup down a little too hard. "I'm sure your team was happy to see you."

I shifted on the chair under Dad's questioning stare. "They're still cool and all. But come on, Dad. We both know I'm not gonna play ghostball again." I slid a bite of pancake into my mouth but barely tasted it.

"We don't know that." Dad set down his fork and looked at me. "The doctors said not now. That doesn't mean not ever."

I pushed my plate away. "I don't want to play."

Dad's eyes widened.

"You? Not play ghostball? Are you serious?" Jason swallowed a large piece of pancake and nearly choked.

"No. I don't. It reminds me too much—" I swallowed the knot in my throat. "Things change." I'd changed. And I didn't want to be anyone's hero. Not anymore.

Dad looked at me, but I stared at my plate wishing Jason would say something funny. Syrup puddled temptingly in the middle of one of my pancakes, but I couldn't eat it. Mom used to make the Saturday morning pancakes, but Dad said he'd keep the tradition going. His were almost as good as hers.

Dad ate the last bite from his plate, but didn't lick the syrup from his fork like he used to. "Well, perhaps we can discuss this again after your next checkup. You might change your mind."

"Maybe," I said, but knew I wouldn't.

Dad cleared his throat. "What about you, Jason? Are you still playing?"

Now it was Jason's turn to squirm under Dad's firing-squad gaze. "Um . . . well, no."

"Right." Dad, clearly unhappy he couldn't use Jason as motivation for me to rejoin the team, looked back at me. "Well maybe you'll have fun today."

"What'd you mean?" Jason and I asked together.

"Hannah's birthday party, remember?" He stood and dug through a plastic bag on the counter. "I have no idea what twelve-year-old girls like so I asked the clerk." Dad pulled a large stuffed pink chinchilla with a polka-dotted bow tie out of the bag.

Jason nearly choked on his pancake again and I tried to hide my wince.

Dad held the stuffed animal at arm's length. "What? You don't think she'll like it?" He studied the fuzzy creature. "Maybe I should've asked Trudy," he mumbled.

Just then, Mrs. Wilson appeared beside me, her face inches from the chinchilla. "Oh, how a-dorable. She'll love it."

"Naw, it's great, Mr. Lenard." Jason nearly spit his pancake across the room with one snorting laugh, but he managed to hold back.

I ignored the fat phantom and Jason, and kept talking to Dad. "I don't know. I don't know her that well. And she's changed. But I'm sure it'll be fine." It will go great with her paranormal investigator stuff.

"Watch your tone there, young man. You are speaking to your father." With her hands on her hips and her cheeks puffed out, I struggled to keep a straight face, but there was no way I was going to give her attention. Even if she was real.

"Well, if there'd been more time, I would've let you pick something out." Dad glanced at the kitchen clock. "As it is, we've only got two hours."

"It starts at noon?" I absolutely did not want to go to my Pretender cousin's birthday party.

"Ooo, a birthday party. Sounds like fun." Jason rolled his eyes, took the last pancake off the plate, and shoved it in his mouth. "Let me know how that goes." He looked at his watch. "Sorry I can't make it. I gotta help my dad." He grinned at me and waved before disappearing through the back door, which closed with a creaky thud.

Dad nodded. "Right, so chop-chop. Go toss in a load of laundry, shower, do whatever it is you need to do and get ready to go."

I shoved one last, large bite of fluffy heaven into my mouth and wished I was too sick to go to a party.

White and silver balloons decorated the doorway to Hannah's house and ghostly gray streamers fluttered along the white porch railing. This was my first visit there since my aunts and Hannah moved in two months ago.

A willowy, wavy head of brown hair came into view on the front porch of the old Victorian. Aunt Elena. I hadn't seen her since I was eight. Dad said they'd all come to visit me at the hospital, but I don't remember it. She hunched over the floorboards, painting a large protection seal on the aging wood. A Third Pentacle of Jupiter dangled from a chain on her neck and there were several other Seals of Solomon that I couldn't make out.

She set down her paintbrush as we reached the front door. "Chris, Alex," she said, her voice so low it might have been the wind. "Excuse the paint. One can't be too careful to ensure our sigils are sound."

"Right," Dad said, not even bothering to hug his sister. I couldn't blame him. Who would be painting sigils in front of a house during a birthday party?

Her gaze snagged on me, her green eyes piercing. "My, Alex, you've grown."

I shivered and scooted away, half hiding on the other side of Dad, wishing I was anywhere else.

Dad hurried to ring the doorbell.

"Hello," a cheerful voice rang out and my aunt Trudy, now sporting dyed red hair, opened the front door. Last time I'd seen her—about two years ago—her hair had been brown. Just like Dad's and Elena's. I guess having Uncle David leave her had caused her to make some changes. I didn't really like this one.

She hugged Dad like she hadn't seen him in years. "I'm so glad you came, Chris." She smiled at me. "Hello, Alex. You're looking really— well."

"Um, thanks," I said, wondering if she'd seen me in the hospital when I was out of my mind on pain meds. I thought I remembered her being there talking to Dad.

Aunt Trudy showed us inside. I hadn't really known our old neighbors and had never been inside this house, so I was curious. A long wooden staircase lay in front of us, and right past that lay a dimly lit front room with an attached kitchen and dining area where a small group of gray-headed people stood mumbling over a bowl of punch. It looked more like a funeral than a girl's birthday party.

"Um . . ." Every nerve in my body screamed at me to bolt.

"Hi." Hannah's smiling face and hoot-owl eyes emerged from the sea of gray heads. "I'm so glad you came."

As much as I wished I wasn't there, I couldn't help feeling a little sorry for Hannah. Who'd want a birthday party like this? Where were all the other kids, anyway? Never mind. She was twelve, not ten. And being new here I guess she didn't have any friends to invite.

Dad handed the oversized gift bag to Hannah. "Happy birthday."

Oh, no. I looked around, desperately seeking for a place to hide.

Hannah yanked the pink tissue paper from the bag, stuck in her hand, and pulled out the massive fur ball.

Her nose wrinkled, but she tried to keep the grimace from her face. "Ah—thanks," she said to Dad. "I, uh, I've always wanted a chinchilla."

Dad squirmed, but Aunt Trudy dragged him away from the embarrassment. I wished I could've been dragged away with him.

I stared at my feet, then at the mammoth chinchilla partially blocking Hannah's face. "Um . . ."

"Let me guess . . . your dad picked it out?" Hannah smirked.

"Pretty much." I cringed, shoving my hands deep into my pockets. At least Hannah was my cousin and not some cute girl from school. This was bad enough.

"Well, come on, then." She held the chinchilla with one hand and tugged on my arm with the other.

"Where are we going?"

"To put him in my room." She led me down a hallway already covered in school photos of Hannah. She looked almost like a regular kid in her younger photos—regular glasses, regular shirts. But the last few photos she'd changed to black shirts with the black, bug-eye glasses. We stopped at the last door on the left.

I peered in the open doorway, taking in the decor: silver sigils glittered on the windows, classification posters of ghosts and a diagram of the seven planes of existence hung on the walls, along with another poster of Edgar Allan Poe. Definitely nothing pink. If I remembered, her last room had been bright yellow. I wondered what had happened to make her go so dark.

Hannah placed the oversized, pink fur ball in the center of her dark gray bed. "There." She positioned his puffy tail and turned to face me. "Well, he certainly adds some color."

"Uh . . ." My cheeks burned and I hoped they weren't the same color as Hannah's new rodent friend.

"Don't worry about it, Alex. I'm just glad you're here." Her voice dipped sadly, like maybe she'd never be happy again.

"Well, happy birthday." I shrugged and wondered when in Solomon's name I'd gotten so uncomfortable around Hannah.

"Thanks." Hannah looked around her room, her face uncertain, then she gave a tiny nod, and pulled down the paranormal investigator kit she'd taken for her class presentation. She laid the gray case on the edge of her bed.

Drat it all. Why'd she have to bring that out? I shuffled into the room and glanced down at her box of ghostly goodies.

"So you really want to be an investigator?" I asked. A wave of nervousness at the thought rippled over me. The last time I'd seen her, she'd never so much as said the word ghost.

Hannah's face lit up. "Sure I do. Think of it—helping the psychics find trapped spirits. Helping keep people safe. Psychics aren't the bad guys, you know?" She popped open the kit. "Besides, the OPI is too busy to handle most low-level spirits and there simply aren't enough psychics in town to deal with them either. Aunt Elena really thinks paranormal investigators will be a huge part of taking care of the Problem if people give them a chance."

"Last time I saw you, I thought you wanted to be a doctor."

"Things changed after Dad left." She shrugged.

I guess I knew what she meant. Her dad hadn't been killed; her parents had just gotten divorced, but still, her dad was out of her life. Gone. My mom was gone. Maybe we did have something in common. I scanned the kit, recalling that the black handheld device with a digital readout was an EMF detector. I also saw a temperature gauge, a motion detector, and a recording device. "What's this thing called again?" I pointed to a beige box with a set of attached headphones. Untouched didn't need to know about paranormal investigative equipment. We simply had to know our basic sigils and wards.

"An EVP listener. Electronic voice phenomena," Hannah reminded me.

"Right." Would that thing actually pick up Mrs. Wilson's voice, if there really were a Mrs. Wilson? If it could, then I'd know for sure if I was crazy or if something had gone tragically wrong with my brain. "Do you—do you really think it'll work?"

Hannah gave a half shrug, but her eyes danced with excitement. "I sure hope so. Guess we'll find out tonight."

"What's tonight?"

"Aunt Elena's leading a team to investigate a house that was built in the 1820s. The current owner can't sell it. They say it's haunted."

I fought back a shiver and held my breath to stop the panic rising in my chest. The Untouched lived among ghosts, but we certainly didn't seek them out. I let out a long, slow breath. "How'd you even get into this stuff?"

Hannah's eyes flickered to the floor. "When my dad left, Aunt Elena moved in with us. She's a Class C Psychic so the Office of Psychic Intervention wouldn't hire her. And the town psychics in Boston said she's not powerful enough. So, she's found a way to use her gift by combining it with paranormal investigation. She was one of the best PIs in Boston, and she'll be the best here. Aunt Elena is beginning to prove that PIs can be useful in dealing with the Problem." Hannah twisted her hair around her finger. "As for why I got into it? Well, at first it distracted me from missing my dad. Then I really started to like it. It sort of—I don't know—it sort of feels right. So, I help her out on investigations whenever I can."

Hannah opened a pack of batteries and put them in the EVP listener. "These tools are good. Definitely useful, but it's best to have a good psychic on the team."

"So Elena is really psychic?" Dad always pegged Aunt Elena as a Pretender. Mom had talked with her when she was doing research on certain topics, but she'd never said much about it since the government didn't officially recognize paranormal investigators as part of a solution to the ghost Problem; Dad wanted me to keep away from psychics. Learning the history of occult and basic wards was good enough for him. He was never thrilled with Mom's job. He'd only tolerated it because he loved her so much.

Three months ago I would have run away from my cousin and this conversation. Three months ago my life had been ghostball and video games and having buddies over for pizza. Three months ago I still had Mom. Now it was just me and Dad and my formerly estranged family.

And Ms. Wilson.

So, I didn't run. I stayed.

"Aunt Elena's a little psychic," Hannah went on. "She can't really predict when she'll hear or see things, which makes her gift a bit unreliable. She sure did like talking with your mom, though. I'm sorry about what happened."

"Uh, thanks," I said and stared at my feet, and an awkward silence filled the room.

"I'm surprised you don't know more about this PI stuff since your mom worked with occult history."

"I didn't really care." Okay, that sounded harsh. "I mean, it wasn't my thing like it is yours, you know? She was just Mom. And that was her job. Like, it was what she did at work. We didn't talk about it much at home." Now I was babbling, but I was in too deep. "I didn't pay much attention to it. You know, like you're not all into teeth just because your parent's a dentist. Sort of like that. So, I don't 'know all about' anything." I kind of trailed off.

"I get it. I'm really into my aunt's work, is all." She shrugged. "I think I can really make a difference helping her with what she does."

"That's a good thing, I guess. Especially if it helped distract you from your dad."

Now it was Hannah's turn to squirm. "Yeah. I'm so glad she's putting her skills to use and letting me help. I really do like it. Still, I'd love to work with someone who is gifted with clairaudience."

"Clair—what?" I asked.

"Being able to hear them." She gestured around the room. "You know—spirits. Clairaudients hear ghosts. Clairsentients feel them. They can get a sensation of what the spirit is feeling or what they went through when they died. Clairscents can smell things from the spirit realm that aren't here in the physical world. There are lots of clair senses, but that's not my point. I was talking about psychic investigators and the government. The OPI handles the scary ghosts and demons and such, but the lost, harmless spirits are often left to wander. They're part of the Problem, even if they don't cause a fuss. The Untouched don't even know they exist. It's kinda sad, really."

Bingo. Mrs. Wilson, she totally had to be one of those kinds of spirits—if she were real. The harmless kind.

I thought of my mom visiting me in my hospital room, something I'd been trying hard not to think of until now. Could Mom be a nice wandering spirit? Was she lost and stuck here? I swallowed back the knot in my throat and touched the blazing blue Nazar Boncuğu amulet she'd given me in the hospital. No. She gave me her necklace and told me she loved me and moved on. She had no reason to stay. I was freaking out over nothing. "I don't want to meddle. I'd rather live my life and leave the ghosts to the professionals." Great. Now I was starting to sound like Dad.

"You're just as bad as the kids at school." She snapped her paranormal investigation kit closed.

"Excuse me?" I scowled and headed out of her room. "I'm not anything like them." Maybe I used to be, but not anymore. Kids at school could be jerks. I was not a jerk. And I was not some psychic freak.

"Alex—wait." She chased me out into the hall. "I'm sorry . . . It's just that no one at school here understands. I—I know I'm different. And I used to care what kids thought. Like really care. I tried to look normal and act normal, but then Dad left and none of that mattered anymore. I don't know . . . I guess after he left I started focusing on things that are important to me." She sniffed back tears and my gut churned with guilt. "Back at my old school a few kids got it, and so did some of my teachers, even if they thought I was weird. Ms. Grimes only tolerates me when I talk about PI stuff and she's an occult history teacher." She lifted her shoulders up, then dropped them. "The kids here think I'm a Pretender for being an Untouched and still being interested in anything beyond our basic wards. They don't understand what PIs can do."

I dropped my eyes to my shoes, not wanting her to know I'd thought the same thing. Wishing—just a little bit—that I didn't care so much about what other people thought. And maybe paranormal investigators really could help with the Problem. I know Dad had to wait for weeks sometimes to get the town psychics to clear a house of a harmless, but noisy spirit.

"It's not like I can't hear the whispers." Hannah stepped in front of me, forcing me to meet her eyes. "I know I'm different, but I'm not a Pretender. I don't know . . . I guess I just figured with your mom, well, with what she did, I figured maybe you'd be different?"

Her question hung in the thickening air. But what was I supposed to say? Yeah, I'm different now because of an accident that killed my mom and tore up my hip? And I'll never play ghostball again. Yeah, I'm different now because I may actually be seeing ghosts. I couldn't say that. Dad would have me committed. Everybody knows if you're not psychic by age ten, then you're not going to be psychic. Ever. I'm no exception. And there was no way a car accident could make it happen, right?

"Well, I'm not," I snapped, letting the anger of my destroyed life out in three words.

Hannah's face crumpled, tears filling her brown eyes.

Shame and anger welled up inside. I shouldn't have snapped at her. She didn't cause the accident or destroy my life. But the last thing I needed was my weirdo cousin I barely knew trying to make things even worse. Especially not when she made a hobby of chasing ghosts while all I wanted to do was escape the thought of them.

"Did you invite Alex to come along on the investigation tonight?" A calm female voice startled me from the doorway.

I flinched. Aunt Elena's cool green eyes stabbed into mine.

"Aunt Elena." Hannah shouldered her way past me and gave her a hug. "No. I didn't invite him. He doesn't want to know more. He's just like the rest of them."

Aunt Elena's gaze lingered on me a little too long. "Oh, I don't know about that, dear one. I think he'd quite like to come along."

Susan McCauley

CHAPTER FIVE

D ad," I pleaded. "I don't want to stay with Aunt Trudy and Hannah. I'll be fine at home. I'm not afraid." I watched Mrs. Wilson do a pirouette across the front room rug and inwardly shuddered. "I'll call Jason. We can stay here and play video games or something."

"I thought Jason had to help his dad?"

My shoulders fell. "Oh, I forgot." Playing video games with Jason sounded so much better than being forced to hang out with my aunts and my wannabe psychic cousin.

"I didn't expect these sales to come through so quickly. I have to make sure the town psychic is there to approve and reinforce the wards and sigils before the new owners can sign. And I need these sales. We need these sales," he said pointedly. Of course we did. Dad had said it more than once, even with his high sales, my medical bills and Mom's funeral expenses after the car accident had far exceeded anything he'd thought possible. "I have to go to the office and do some paperwork. I'll be home by nine o'clock. We can still watch a show."

"But why do I have to stay with them? What if Aunt Elena starts in on the paranormal investigation stuff?" Of all things, that was the last thing Dad would want me talking about. He hated psychic stuff. "You never even wanted me to go to Mom's office to see paranormal artifacts when she was alive—" I let that last word die in my mouth.

Mrs. Wilson stopped dancing, her eyes bouncing from me to Dad.

Dad stiffened and shoved a file into his tattered briefcase. "I don't want you home alone so soon after the accident. What if something happens? What if you fall and need help getting up? That's part of why they moved here. To be close to family. To help."

I was injured, not helpless.

"I talked it over with Trudy. She says they'd love to have you. And—if Elena discusses her . . . work . . . well, maybe learning more about what's behind the paranormal will help put an end to your concerns."

"But—"

Dad held up his hand. "No buts. Dr. Midgley told me you thought you talked with your Mom's spirit."

"But I—" My voice rose a notch.

"I'm your father and he thought I should know." Dad's voice rose over mine.

I itched with betrayal and my face grew hot. I thought that shrink was supposed to keep my secrets. "But you hate psychics," I spat.

"It's what your mom would've done."

We both stood there, equally shocked that we were yelling at each other. I felt tense, like I was locked in some kind of hunched fury. He was right, though, and I knew it. Mom would've said, "Gather information. Information is power." Dad did hate psychics, but he loved Mom. So did I.

Still do.

Dad put his hands on my shoulders. His body seemed to go limp and all the fight went out of his voice. "Look, son, I want you to get better. Not just your hip—all of you. As much as I don't like what the psychics did to our world—to the very essence of our existence . . ."

Uh, oh, I felt an antipsychic lecture coming on—like the ones he used to give Mom at dinner when she talked with nonstop excitement about meeting with a psychic about some occult object that was supposed to be imbued with power.

But Dad just sighed and shook his head. "Like them or not, psychics are a necessary evil. And I suppose PIs are, too. Maybe Elena will remind you that you can't see or hear ghosts if you're Untouched. And you are Untouched." Without another word he snatched up his leather briefcase and headed out the front door.

Mrs. Wilson's eyebrows drew together in concern. "No wonder you won't talk to me. He won't think you're a psychic; he'll think you're insane."

I started to talk, then stopped myself. I would not respond to my hallucination.

"Don't worry, child. He'll come around." Mrs. Wilson gave my shoulder an icy pat that felt way too real to be a hallucination. "And after tonight, I'm sure you will, too."

Well, of course, no sooner had Dad left then Aunt Trudy called claiming she had a migraine. Personally, I think she drank too much at Hannah's party. But she told me that I was to go and spend the evening with Aunt Elena and Hannah to help with the investigation. "Meet them at Elena's office at six o'clock," she'd said.

That was the last thing I wanted to do. Go on a ghost hunt. Besides, Dad had gone to work, so how would he know if I stayed home or not? I flopped back on the sofa and grabbed the controller, etched with a Third Pentacle of Jupiter and Sixth Pentacle of Mars, both pentacles inscribed with Hebrew and a verse from Psalms. One could never be too cautious when using electronics. Spirits loved traveling through wires, which is probably why the city still used gas lamps and petrol for all of our ground transportation. We even had backup gas lamps at school in case of an "incident." Our homes and offices had electricity, but it was monitored. One refrigerator, one washing machine, one dryer, and one TV per household. And every electric machine was required by law to be etched with the Third Pentacle of Jupiter. More seals were better, but also more expensive. I flipped on the TV and selected the gaming option.

Mrs. Wilson plopped down beside me and watched intently. "My boy Jamie used to play those games."

I tried to ignore her, but my fingers stiffened on the remote.

"I'd almost forgotten . . . He'd get home from school, toss his backpack there by the door, then flip on the Atari until homework and dinner." She gave a sigh that almost made me feel bad for her. "Oh, I miss my Jamie."

Translucent tears glistened on her cheek and she sniffed. "Ah well." She reached toward me, sending shivers shooting across my skin, and I leapt off the sofa. "We must live in the present. The here and now, right? Why don't you be a good boy and turn on Wheel of Fortune for me?"

That was it. She'd nearly touched me again. I flipped off the video game and flipped on Wheel of Fortune. Maybe I did need to go back to Dr. Midgley. What would he say if he knew I was putting on a television show for what he called a hallucination? I touched Mom's amulet for luck and tried to clear my mind. She would want me to go. I headed for the front door and grabbed my jacket.

"Have a good evening, Alex," she called. "Be careful out there—"

I shut the door on her. I couldn't take it. I could not hear ghosts. I could not see ghosts. I could not feel ghosts. I was tested at ten like everybody else in the world and it was determined that I am not a psychic. I had to be nuts. So I'd go and be nuts with some paranormal investigators and they could prove to me that I was hallucinating.

With a shove, the garage door creaked open. I took my bike from the corner, praying my leg would still pedal, and, with a few pumps, I shot down the sidewalk. My hip hurt, but I could still ride.

I slowed as I reached the wrought-iron gates of Lafayette Cemetery No. 1. Dad had promised to take me to visit her grave when I was ready. I still wasn't ready.

Guilt gnawed at me, but I pushed it away and headed downtown. Historic brick buildings surrounded me and the last winds of summer sent goose bumps coursing along my arms. I shivered then pedaled harder. I needed to get there and have their equipment show nothing while I saw some ghost and proved that I'm a crazy hallucinator instead of a crazy psychic. Crazy hallucinators could be fixed, right? This was all some sort of accident-induced psychosis and I simply needed time to heal like Dr. Midgley'd said.

I hopped off my bike, walked it across a well-worn street of the French Quarter, inhaling the sweet, warm, mouthwatering smell of beignets. Dad, Jason, and I needed to make a trip to Café Du Monde. I hadn't had a beignet in months. I scanned the numbers until I found the 900 block. Above the office hung a wooden sign inscribed with gold lettering: Elena's Paranormal Investigation Services. I'd probably passed this storefront hundreds of times, but had never imagined my own aunt would set up shop here. I peeked through the wide glass window. Gold leaf-furnishings, unpacked boxes, and stacks of paranormal gear lined the glass storefront etched with glittering sigils.

My heart pounded against my ribs. I didn't even want to see my old friends, let alone hang out with family I hardly knew. Maybe I should find a coffee shop and get a mug of hot chocolate. I'd call Dad, tell him where I was, and then I'd go back and see Dr. Midgley.

The same Dr. Midgley who'd told Dad my secrets. Told him I'd seen Mom.

I held on to Mom's Nazar Boncuğu, wishing I'd died right along with her. The amulet slipped through my fingers and found a resting place against my chest. I was either crazy or seeing ghosts, and I didn't need Dr. Midgley to find out. I'd have to do it on my own. So, I stretched my hand toward the door.

"Alex?" Hannah's cool voice glided up next to me, and I turned to face her. Her lips were set somewhere between a smile and a frown. "I'm surprised you actually came."

"I didn't have much of a choice, did I?" I growled without meaning to.

She pushed open the door to Aunt Elena's office, paranormal kit in hand. "I suppose it's always good to have a skeptical Untouched on the team. That way when you see our evidence for the first time and you pee your pants, I can catch it on tape." She grinned evilly.

I followed her in, bike in tow, aiming daggers at the back of her head. Pee my pants? Really?

Aunt Elena sat at a circular table toward the back of the store poring over some notes. "Alex, why don't you put your bike there?" She motioned to a spot on the wall between a bookcase and a stack of boxes, then gestured for me to sit in a chair beside her.

I leaned my bike against the wall. "I'd rather stand."

"We'll be waiting until the rest of the team arrives." She glanced at my left leg. "Your hip might feel better if you sit. We'll be on our feet a lot during the investigation."

"My hip's fine." It wasn't. It still hurt. Not the intense, nearly unbearable pain I'd had right after the accident. Or the equally excruciating pain after the surgeries. This was bearable, but persistent. A pain that wouldn't let me forget.

Aunt Elena's expression commanded me into the chair. "Sit, Alex. Save your leg."

I huffed and flopped into the seat.

Hannah set her investigator case on the table and flipped the lid open.

"All ready to go?" Aunt Elena asked.

Hannah studied the instruments, eyes bigger than an owl's and bright with excitement. "I think so. New batteries. The wards are government certified and the sigils are sound. Everything checked out when I tested them."

"Good." Aunt Elena swung around to me. "We're waiting for Frank to join us. You can help Hannah with her equipment. I'd like to capture EVPs if possible. And if Hannah's gear can confirm what we get with Frank's then that'll be even better." She gave Hannah a wink. "Let's show this town what we can do."

A tinkling bell rang and a man with dark hair and graying temples strode in. His sleeves were rolled up, so I couldn't help but notice the black ink tattoos covering his forearms. In artistic script were tattooed seals of protection, along with sigils in Hebrew, and a massive gargoyle that was so lifelike it looked as if it'd fly off the guy's arm and attack me at any moment.

Whoa. And I thought sigiled T-shirts were overkill. This guy took spiritual precautions to a whole new level.

"That's Frank Martinez. He's famous," Hannah whispered with awe and shoved her glasses farther up the bridge of her nose as if it would help her see him more clearly. "Not only is he a Class A Psychic, but he's captured more EVP and infrared hits than any other investigators on the East Coast. He's got full-spectrum infrared cameras in his bag."

A Class A Psychic? Here? Real psychics alone were rare enough. But Class A Psychics were almost nonexistent. If I remembered correctly from my fifth-grade paranormal studies class, psychics made up less than 4 percent of the world's population and Class A Psychics made up less than 1 percent of all of them. "If he's a Class A, then what's he doing here with paranormal investigators?"

"He's a retired federal psychic. The OPI still has him consult on investigations. He believes, like Aunt Elena, that combining paranormal investigation techniques and psychic awareness is more powerful than either on its own. Most psychics don't think that way. They're too stuck up to work with us. But not Frank. That's why he's one of the best. He thinks outside the box," she whispered. "Frank and Elena are friends. He's glad she's finally moved here, and has promised to go with us on some of the more interesting cases. Together we're going to change the way the world sees PIs."

I rolled my eyes, but didn't let Hannah see. We'd been dealing with the Problem for over a hundred years, and she thought they were going to change things? Talk about ambitious.

"Frank." Aunt Elena gestured to the retired OPI psychic, then to me. "This is my nephew, Alex. He'll be assisting Hannah with her new equipment."

Frank's eyes washed over me and I had the unnerving feeling he knew what I'd been going through.

"He's our team skeptic," Hannah added with a cool toss of tangled hair. "He's not too sure about investigators, and like a typical Untouched, he's afraid of ghosts."

"I'm not afraid of ghosts."

"You should be." Frank had caught me in my lie.

I closed my mouth. Okay, so maybe I was afraid. Mrs. Wilson wasn't scary—if she was even real—but that shot-up janitor scared me. All Untouched were afraid of ghosts. It's probably why we were scared of psychics. I didn't want to be a psychic. It'd be better to be crazy.

We rode in Aunt Elena's not-so-gently used SUV; amulets hung from the rearview mirror and sigils covered the windows and doors. And I'd thought Mom was paranoid, which I guess made sense, considering how much she knew about the occult. Still, Aunt Elena made Mom's sigils and wards look tame.

"It's all-wheel drive and dual purpose." Aunt Elena had laughed when I climbed in, eyeing her amulets. "I can haul PIs, investigation equipment, kids, bicycles." She winked at me and Hannah in the rearview mirror.

After a short ride past the library and donut shop, Frank following us in his own warded, white van, Aunt Elena slowed to a stop in front of a house Dad would have called Greek Revival style. Its wide front porch and slender columns invited us into a yawning mouth of a door.

Gazing up at its eye-like second-story windows, I cringed, not sure if the flash of shadow I'd glimpsed was a mirage from the setting sun or my imagination.

Don't freak out. It's just a hallucination.

Aunt Elena opened the SUV's tailgate. "Come on, kids. Hop to it. Mr. Barrett said specifically that he wanted the investigation done this weekend and we've got a lot of equipment to unload."

Black T-shirt flapping against her skinny body, Hannah leapt out of the car, obviously having trouble containing her excitement. I didn't move so quickly. I could always blame it on my leg. I opened the car door and warm, muggy air wrapped itself around me. Ignoring the sweat already beginning to form on my back, I swung one leg out and climbed stiffly to my feet.

After we spent a frenzied hour of setting up tables, cameras, and an array of paranormal paraphernalia on the front porch, the sun had set and inky darkness filled in the evening sky.

"Frank, you have the infrareds?"

"Check." Frank secured a large Nazar Boncuğu with a Third Pentacle of Jupiter etched in its center around his neck and flipped a switch on his camera.

I touched my own amulet and looked up to find Frank staring at me, a slight frown on his scruffy face. "I'm sorry about your mother. She was a top-rate occult academic. I read all her work."

"You knew my mother?" Wow. How could she have been so well-connected in the psychic world and be married to my dad?

Frank shook his head. "I met her a couple times at OPI headquarters when she gave presentations, but I didn't know her well. Just her work."

I swallowed my disappointment. Mom's amulet slipped through my fingers and rattled against my collarbone. Maybe it was better he hadn't known her. Dad would've probably flipped out if she'd had a Class A Psychic for a friend. And I would be even more miserable having someone around me to remind me of what I'd lost. I scratched at the nagging wound on my hip. Right. As if I needed reminding.

"Hannah, turn on your EVP meter and camcorder. We're going in." Aunt Elena took a deep breath. "I'll see what I can pick up. If anyone else feels or hears anything, investigate it. We'll handle crossing it to the other side. You kids stay together. I'll be the floater. I'll start with Frank. Hannah, if you or Alex need me, just holler."

Hannah bobbed her head and grinned like a demented jack-o'-lantern.

How she could be so giddy was beyond me. What did she get out of chasing ghosts? I swallowed and shoved down the sense of swirling pressure that had invaded my chest. I had to do this. I had to prove I was seeing hallucinations, not ghosts.

Aunt Elena went inside first, followed by Frank and Hannah. I brought up the rear, closing the door with a soft click behind me.

"We'll take upstairs," said Frank, his voice sharp against the silence. "You two work the downstairs."

Frank climbed toward the rooms upstairs, Aunt Elena trailing behind.

The air was silent and still, save for the faint buzz coming from Hannah's equipment and her gentle breathing. In and out. In and out. Nope, no ghosts here. The machine would register if there were. I must've hallucinated the shadow in the window because the machines indicated nothing.

My heartbeat started to slow and I took in my surroundings. The house was still furnished, but sparsely. A Victorian sofa faced the brick fireplace and an old, wooden bookcase sat against one wall. It smelled of dust and mold and decay.

"This way," Hannah said, and I followed her toward a large sitting area. She panned her EVP reader back and forth, leading us closer to an open doorway that led to the kitchen.

That's when I felt it. A strange surge of energy, like a small riptide at the beach, tugged at me. I stopped dead in the middle of the room, the feeling urging me to a closed door.

I moved toward the door, one leaden foot following the other. It was as if my feet didn't belong to me; a numb, dull pull coaxed me closer. Closer and closer until I reached out my hand. My fingers grazed the bronze doorknob. It barely moved.

A skeleton key stuck out from a gaping keyhole. I reached forward, hoping it was rusted shut. No such luck. It unlocked and the door squeaked open, the key coming free in my hand. I slipped it in my pocket and peered down the tunnel-like stairwell into the darkness, descending toward the bowels of the house.

"Alex . . . look at this old—" I barely registered Hannah's voice. "Alex, where in Solomon's name are you?"

I couldn't go to her. Wouldn't. Something had taken hold of me. I didn't want to, but I knew I had to go down there. Down. Into the dark. I had to find out what was there.

"Alex, come on. Let's do this level first, then we can check out the basement."

But I didn't answer. Instead, I took another step into the darkness.

"Oh, for heaven's sake. Fine. I'll follow you," Hannah snapped.

I was already on the stairs, descending into the depths of the house, when I heard breathing.

And it wasn't Hannah.

Hannah flipped a switch on the wall behind me.

Click.

Click.

Click.

Click.

She flicked the switch on and off, but nothing happened, so she turned on her camcorder light, nearly blinding me.

"Help me. Oh, please help me." A hollow voice echoed through the basement walls. "Is anyone there? Can anyone hear me?"

I stopped on the stairs and listened, cold sweat breaking out on my forehead. I swallowed the baseball-sized lump of fear forming in my throat, the pressure in my chest squeezing tighter. "Can you hear that?" My voice sounded strangled, choked.

"Hear what?" Hannah hefted the camera up and aimed it at me.

The light blazed in my face. "Stop it," I snapped, shielding my eyes with my hand.

She kept filming. "No way. It's part of evidence collection. And if you see or hear anything I'm capturing it on tape."

"Oh, please. I know someone's there. Please. Help me. I'm trapped. Oh, no. He's coming . . . He's—" The hollow voice cut off.

I took a shallow gasp and turned away from Hannah and her camera. "Please . . ." My voice sounded frightened, but I couldn't help it. I was scared. Scared of the pleading voice. Scared that I wasn't hallucinating. Scared that all this was way too real. "Turn that thing off. It's blinding me."

Hannah snorted. "Oh, all right." She flipped off the camcorder light. "Take this." She handed me her EMF reader. "I'm going to get Frank and Elena."

"But—" I fumbled with the EMF reader. I had no idea how to use this thing. "We're not supposed to split up."

Too late. Hannah sprinted up the stairs, leaving me alone in the dark basement with the terrified voice.

And the machine had captured it.

Hannah leapt into the backseat of the SUV next to me, making the leather squeak.

"You heard something." Hannah hooted at me. "I know you did."

I sat there, numbly staring into the distance. Away from the house. Away from my cousin who cared more about EVPs than me.

"Oh, Alex, come on . . . I mean, you've got to tell us—" Hannah begged.

Aunt Elena shut the passenger-side door, climbed in, and closed her own door. "Hannah. Not now." The frown in Aunt Elena's voice was clear, but also mixed with excitement. "He'll talk to us when he's ready."

Hannah huffed and fell back into her seat. A pout pursed her lips, but I didn't care. What I'd seen . . . what I'd felt. I trembled and tried to shake off the woman's desperation. I didn't want any part of it. I didn't want any part of their investigation or this house.

"I just want to go home," I implored Aunt Elena through the rearview mirror. "Please. Take me home."

She looked at me for a moment as if she wanted to say something, but changed her mind. Finally, she nodded and put the SUV in drive.

That's when I made the mistake of looking up at the house. Silhouetted against an upstairs window, looking straight at me, was the outline of a man.

Ten minutes later, I limped into my house, shut the front door, and locked it. The hall clock read 9:30 p.m. Dad still wasn't home. So much for him not wanting me to be alone. I wished Mom were here. My heart warped painfully at the thought.

I rushed up the stairs, two at a time, ignoring my grumbling stomach and the throb in my left hip. I wanted to be alone. Alone with my shame. Alone with my grief. Alone with my fear.

I locked my bedroom door, crawled into bed, and wept. Not just the rain-like tears that fell when I usually thought of Mom, but the thunderstorm kind of tears that shake your body and rattle your bones. The kind that wring out your soul.

Racking sobs shook my body and I gasped for breath. If only I hadn't made it into the ghostball championships, then Mom wouldn't have been driving me to that game. Then we wouldn't have been in that accident. She'd be here. With me. Alive. And I wouldn't have almost died and now be able to see ghosts. None of this would be happening.

"Oh, Mom." I took a stuttering breath and pressed my snotty face against the hot, damp pillow. "Why did you have to die?"

A gentle weight settled on the bed next to me.

I stiffened, but didn't care who heard me crying.

A cool hand caressed the back of my head. Almost like Mom had done when I'd been sad or ill or injured.

Tears still warm on my cheeks, I raised my face from the pillow. It was Mrs. Wilson. She looked down at me with the kindest, gentlest expression. My tears kept flowing.

"Shhhh, now. It's going to be all right, honey," her New Orleans drawl warm and comforting, even as she put her cold arm around me, somehow managing to keep it from sinking through my shirt. "I know it's hard. I do. But your mom's at peace. I'm sure she is or I'd have seen her here."

I hadn't wanted to talk to Mrs. Wilson. I hadn't wanted to acknowledge her presence. But if she knew about Mom . . . if she knew about ghosts. I grimaced. How could I be psychic? I'd been tested. I was too old. I was Untouched, wasn't I?

Something hard pressed against my hip and I remembered the key in my pocket. The key that had led me into the depths of that house. In my fright, I'd forgotten to put it back in the basement door. I pulled it out of my pocket, feeling its cold weight in my palm, before setting it on the night table next to my bed. I wasn't a crazy hallucinator. I was a crazy psychic. And there wasn't a fix for that.

Maybe I needed someone who would understand. Not Dr. Midgley. Not Dad. Not most of the world who believed if you weren't a psychic by age ten, you'd always be Untouched. Maybe somehow I was different. Maybe Mrs. Wilson would understand. And maybe, just maybe, she could help me.

I bit the inside of my lip, hard, to make sure I was really awake. The pain confirmed my consciousness, and my stomach did a somersault. Then, I took a deep breath and spoke to my very first ghost.

CHAPTER SEVEN

I collapsed at the lunchroom table, sloshing the too-runny applesauce out of its puke-green plastic bowl, then glanced at the wall clock. Ugh. Only halfway through Monday and I was Friday-tired.

Jason took a huge bite of a greasy burger, which had been deemed our lunch. I don't know how he was able to eat so much and still be so skinny. I actually carried extra snacks in my backpack in case he got hungry. That's something I'd learned on our third-grade field trip to the science museum when he'd had a massive hunger meltdown—always carry snacks for Jason. I nibbled an edge of my burger and chased it with a gulp of water.

A shadow fell across my tray, eclipsing a brown lump that was supposed to pass for chocolate cake.

"Where you been, Lenard?" Tommy Lord, my old ghostball team captain, stood above me. "The rest of the team's been asking about you. Danny said you're avoiding us."

I stared into my bowl of applesauce, not wanting to have this conversation.

"Look, I know your leg is busted, but, it's like I said the other day, you should still come to practice so you're ready to get back in the game." Tommy's voice softened a little, but I knew he wouldn't leave until I said something.

"I'm not going to get back in the game," I mumbled.

"What are you talking about? You're the best ghostball player this school's had in like fifty years."

I swallowed back all the dread that had led up to this moment. The moment I killed any chance of ever playing ghostball at Rey again. "The bones in my hip shattered." The still-forming scar scratched inside my trousers like it was trying to tell its own story. I ignored it. "I had a total hip replacement. I won't be playing again."

Tommy's face went pale. "Man, I'm so sorry. I had no idea it was that bad." Tommy squirmed, suddenly more uncomfortable than me.

"It's all right." It wasn't, but what was the point in saying so.

"I—we—the team tried to visit you. But your dad kept telling us you didn't want visitors . . . I—I knew about your mom. I had no idea that you . . ."

"Really, Tommy. It's okay. I wasn't in any shape to see you guys." I forced a smile that felt like a grimace.

"Don't worry. I got his back, Tommy," Jason piped up through a mouthful of burger, ending the awkwardness.

Tommy looked at Jason and frowned. "Yeah, well, are you coming back, Anderson? No reason to quit just 'cause Alex isn't going to play."

"Naw, I gotta take care of him." Jason jerked a thumb toward me, then took another bite of burger.

I knew he'd never really liked playing ghostball; he'd rather be out hunting or camping. He'd done it because I asked him to. He'd done it for me. The guys on the team had never understood my friendship with Jason.

"Um, okay . . ." Tommy stood there uncomfortably, looking from Jason to me.

"I'll see ya around, Tommy." I tried to sound as friendly as possible. I didn't want to burn bridges, but there weren't really any bridges to burn. Mine had already collapsed.

"Sure. See ya." Relief flooded Tommy's voice and he disappeared into a pack of ghostball players a few tables over.

"Well that was awkward." Jason slurped down his chocolate milk and eyed my half-eaten burger. "You gonna eat that?"

Suddenly I didn't feel very hungry. "Naw, go ahead."

He reached over and grabbed my burger. "You should drink your milk though. You do need some protein."

"Thanks, Mom—" The word died on my lips and another shadow fell over me. What now?

Hannah sidled up next to us. "Hey, mind if I sit with you guys?" Tray in hands, she plopped down beside me before either of us could reply. "You have to hear what Ms. Grimes said about my essay on paranormal investigation."

Jason groaned, then shoved a few fries in his mouth.

I scowled, but I couldn't turn her away. If I did, she'd probably burst into tears. Or tell my dad. Or both. And, weird or not, she was my cousin. I scooched over a tad to give her more space.

Hannah settled in and placed a napkin on her lap. "Oh, come on. I'm not that bad. It's not my fault most of the kids at this school are so uptight about the paranormal or anyone who's different." She looked at me hard, but I just stared at the greasy, overcooked macaroni 'n' cheese on my plate.

"Besides, we have important things to discuss." She smiled.

"We do?" Jason asked through a partially chewed mouthful of fries.

Hannah wrinkled her nose at him, then took a large bite of lasagna, followed by some salad. "Aunt Elena reviewed the evidence," she whispered, her voice quivering with excitement.

I froze, the sip of milk I'd had nearly curdling in my mouth. She had to bring that up here. Now. Really? I hadn't even told Jason about my crazy ghost-hunting expedition, let alone what I'd heard down in that basement. And there was no way I wanted to tell him about Mrs. Wilson—even if he was the only one who hadn't tried to send me to a therapist. "Can we talk about this later? Like after school?"

"Talk about what?" Jason stopped chewing.

Uh, oh, this was serious. Jason never stopped eating unless he knew something was up.

Hannah's lips pressed together. "I suppose. But Aunt Elena wants you to come to the office after school. And whether or not you want to talk about it, we know you heard something. When you were freaking out—"

"I was not freaking out," I hissed, looking around the cafeteria to be sure no one was listening.

"Freaking out about what?" Jason's voice rose a notch.

"Shhh. Not so loud," I whispered through my teeth. "I'll tell you all about it, J. Later. After school."

Hannah acted like she hadn't heard me. "Oh, whatever. While Alex here's been trying to pretend he couldn't hear a ghost last night, our EMF meter went wild. And we captured an EVP." Her voice twittered with joy. "Aunt Elena says it's the best one she's ever heard."

"I knew it. My best friend is a psychic." Jason slammed his hand on the table, making everyone around us stare. Jason slumped down. "Sorry, X," he whispered, calling me the special Jamaican name he gave me as his best friend. "I knew you weren't crazy when you told me you talked to your mom after the accident."

"Wait. What?" Hannah set down her fork and shoved her glasses up the bridge of her nose so her eyes looked extra-large. "You actually talked to her spirit?"

I shut my eyes and moaned. Why were we having this discussion right now? And why did the Problem even have to exist? "Yes. I saw her. And I talked to her. But I didn't know if she was real or if it was in my head. I've been trying to ignore them, but last night I couldn't."

"Ignore them?" Hannah's voice rose an octave. "You've seen multiple entities?"

My lips pressed shut. Nope. No way was I discussing this any further right now.

"Um, what's an EVP?" Jason shoved a few more fries in his mouth.

"Weren't you listening at all during my presentation? It means electronic voice phenomena." Hannah rattled it out like someone reading from a manual. "I honestly don't know how so many Untouched know so little about the supernatural when we're surrounded by it."

Jason tossed up his hands in surrender. "Okay, that's cool. And, no, I don't know much about paranormal investigation. And, yes, I am Untouched. I only know the wards and sigils I need at home or when I hunt with my dad, but there aren't many ghosts out in the woods." Jason took a final slurp of chocolate milk, crumpled the carton, and tossed it on his tray. "So, what did it say?"

I didn't want to admit it, but I was curious, too.

Hannah's face lit up. "It's a woman's voice. And she said, 'He's coming.'"

I panted in the bathroom, butt against the locked stall, head between my knees. This could not be happening. I gulped in several breaths of toilet air. Stay calm, Alex. Stay calm. Okay, I knew ghosts were real. I talked to Mrs. Wilson last night. But part of me had hoped that the doctors and Dad were right—that I was suffering from some sort of post-traumatic psychosis that would go away. Now I couldn't ignore it. Aunt Elena had proof. On tape. They'd recorded what I'd heard. They'd heard the woman, too. They'd heard her cry out those very same words. He's coming.

A chill ran from my arms up to my head, making the hairs on my scalp prick up.

Deep breaths. In through the nose, out through the mouth—the way the shrink at the hospital had taught me. In through the nose. Out through the mouth. Nice and calm. My pulse slowed and my panic ebbed.

I'd go to Aunt Elena's and see what type of evidence she had. Maybe if I understood it, I'd be able to block them out and stop them from talking to me. Then Dad wouldn't have to know.

I took one more deep breath of stagnant bathroom air, unlocked the stall door, and went to the sink to splash some cool water on my face.

My hand closed around the faucet handle when the bathroom door swung open.

Two of my former teammates, Billy and David, came in, and my stomach did an extra somersault.

"Hey Lenard, where you been?" Billy asked.

"Yeah. Tommy said you're not rejoining the team. What's up?"

Great. Just what I needed. More pressure to rejoin the ghostball team. I pushed off the sink faucet and faced my former teammates. "I'm not."

Billy and David still stood in front of the entrance, faces set in frowns.

"We need you on the team. We don't stand a chance at winning the championship this year without you," Billy said.

"We lost last season because you weren't there." David stuffed his hands in his pockets and scowled.

Yeah, because I was being rushed to the hospital with a broken hip and a dying mother. "It's not like I tried to miss the championship game," I snapped.

Billy held up his hands. "Hey, he didn't mean—"

"I don't care what he meant," I charged on. "Do you have any idea what it's like to be in a massive car wreck? Let alone having your mother die and your hip so torn up you don't even know if you'll walk again?"

"I—" Billy started.

"Don't either of you get it? Life's more than about winning a stupid ghostball championship." I slammed my leg into the bathroom door. Pain burst along my scar and I heard a scream. It took me a second to realize it was my own.

A light fixture exploded above us, raining shattered glass on our heads.

David's and Billy's eyes widened and both backed away from me.

"What was that?" Billy brushed flecks of glass from his hair, his blue eyes flickering around the bathroom.

Silence.

I panted, trying to catch my breath. Trying to stop the throbbing in my scarred hip.

Slowly, one by one, the hot-water faucets turned on—heat and steam fogging up the mirrors.

David's eyes nearly popped out of his head and he ran out the only exit. Billy bolted after him.

I sat up, massaging my throbbing hip, thankful for the disturbance.

The bullet-holed janitor leaned against the far wall, a satisfied smile on his face. "Name's Mr. Thomas, son." He tilted his head by way of greeting. "I know I'm dead. And I know you can see me." He turned off the steaming faucets, one by one. "Thought you could use a distraction just now."

I licked the roof of my mouth, trying to clear the cotton from my tongue. I'd talked to Mrs. Wilson. But I also saw her every day and listened to her every night. I couldn't escape her. I supposed this wasn't much different. "Thanks, but I can handle myself," I said, and stood up unsteadily, brushing shards of glass from my pants.

Mr. Thomas turned off the last faucet and looked me straight in the eye. "Didn't look like it to me, son," he said, his voice soft, his accent southern. "Must be hard for you losin' your mama, and now seein' ghosts and all at a late age, but I'm only tryin' to help."

Guilt took hold and my face grew hot. A kind, Southern black gentleman with bullet holes? Who'd have thought.

"If I didn't care about you kids so much, I wouldn't have stayed. Gettin' more ungrateful every year," Mr. Thomas muttered and disappeared through the bathroom wall.

I tried to wrap my mind around this. Some ghosts were good? Our whole lives the Untouched learned to deflect and protect ourselves from spirits. We were taught to fear them. But some of them actually seemed nice. They were people who'd died and decided not to cross over for one reason or another. Mr. Thomas loved the kids. And Mrs. Wilson kept talking about her son.

A shiver of fear crawled over me like a roach. What about the woman in the wall? And what about the spirit of the evil man who still lurked in that house?

I definitely needed to stop by Aunt Elena's and hear what she had to say. It's not like I'd be offering to go back into the house. Besides, if I didn't go to see the evidence, Jason and Hannah would never let me hear the end of it. And Dad would accuse me of pushing away family. Then it'd be back to the shrink for sure.

I stood up and looked at myself in the still clearing mirrors. "I'll do it." Tomorrow I'd see what kind of evidence Elena found and hear it for myself. But that's it. There was no way any of them were going to get me to go back into that house again.

Chapter Eight

I trudged through the first few leaves of autumn, bright green with hints of orange and yellow—the only ones likely to fall in the warm southern Louisiana weather—and headed for home.

I glanced at my Spellguard watch, the one Mom got me at the last presentation she'd given for the government. It was the safest electronic watch on the planet with sigils inscribed on every gear and battery. And it had a special, nearly invisible seal on the face. A seal that glowed in the dark. It was the same watch that every Paranormal Cybersecurity Squad officer wore, too. Standard issue. Pretty cool. I missed Mom. I could have told her what was happening to me. She would have known what to do. She probably had psychic friends Dad didn't even know about. I still had more than two hours before Dad got home. More than enough time to make dinner. But the last thing I wanted right now was to be home with Mrs. Wilson—alone. She wasn't scary, but, boy, could she be annoying.

I needed time. Time to clear my head. Time to calm my raging heart. Time to think about ghosts without them actually popping up and trying to talk to me. What in Solomon's name was I going to do? If I really was a psychic, and if Dad actually came around, then I might be sent off to some research institute so they could study my brain and find out why I'd come into this ability so late. Not going to happen. There was no way I'd leave my dad or Jason. I'd lost enough already.

I limp-walked down the sidewalk and stopped in front of Lafayette Cemetery No. 1. Great. Not where I needed to be. I didn't want to visit Mom's grave—not yet—and it wasn't exactly the perfect place to escape from ghosts.

Past the wrought-iron fence, among the moss-draped oaks, stood row upon row of mausoleums—those massive stone structures that housed the dead above ground. They had to use them here in New Orleans. When my parents had decided to move back here from Boston when I was six, they'd somehow thought that living in a city that sat below sea level was a good idea. So, most of the bodies had to be buried above ground on account of the high water table and the risk of caskets floating away. A shiver slithered down my spine and stopped me cold. The same cool trail I felt when a ghost was near. I glanced at the maze of tombs and a shadow caught my eye.

A hunched-over, skeletal-looking man speckled with brown liver spots trudged from behind a tree toward an ancient-looking mausoleum. He wasn't translucent, but I swore he must be a ghost.

The man stopped and turned toward me.

I wanted to bolt, but my hip was killing me. And for some weird reason I froze.

The man's murky brown eyes bore into mine, and slowly, very slowly, he lifted a hand and beckoned me closer with a single finger.

My paralyzing fear broke with that gesture, and I turned and hobbled home as fast as I could.

Hip throbbing, I collapsed on the steps of my front porch. I couldn't escape ghosts no matter where I went, could I? Even in the place they were supposed to be dead. Panting, I leaned my head back against one of the white porch columns.

There was no sign of the crooked old man here. Maybe I'd imagined him. I fished out my homework from my backpack. No need to go inside to Mrs. Wilson's mindless yapping just yet. I scribbled out the answers to a few math problems and then pulled out the book assigned by my English teacher: The Graveyard Book. How appropriate. I wondered if Neil Gaiman was really a psychic but pretended not to be so he could write instead of having to hunt spirits. I shoved the book in my backpack. I was not in the mood for more ghosts. Real or imagined.

So, I sat there on the porch in ghost-free bliss and watched the sun drop like an orange globe behind the tree branches, their leaves rustling in the evening breeze. I inhaled the fresh air and shivered. Autumn would be here soon. Maybe I should go inside and get dinner ready.

I checked my Spellguard again. It was nearly half past five. Yup, I'd better go in and make dinner or Dad would know something was wrong. Heaving myself off the porch, I unlocked the front door, dropped my backpack on the hall tree bench, flicked on the light, and froze.

Two inches in front of me stood Mrs. Wilson. She emanated cold. Not her usual chilly breeze that made my skin prickle, but real, lip-numbing cold.

I gasped and jumped back, slamming my shoulder into the edge of the hall tree. "Ouch," I said with a scowl and rubbed away the pain. "Don't do that." I snapped at the pasty ghost, "What's the matter with you?"

She didn't respond, merely stared straight up the stairs. Straight toward my bedroom.

Now what?

Bluish gray and translucent, cold wisps drifted off of her, forming ice on the hall mirror—a look of terror etched in her round, motherly face.

"Uh, Mrs. Wilson?" I waved my hand in front of her.

No reaction. Her gaze remained fixed.

Crazy ghost. I headed for the kitchen.

"Alex—" My name escaped her lips in a hiss.

I stopped at the kitchen doorway and turned to her.

Her eyes were wild like a frightened animal, and her lips trembled. "He's here—" She shrieked and disappeared through the front door.

Fear knotted itself in my chest and I looked up the stairs.

Nothing.

I took a deep breath and pushed away the uneasy feeling trying to take hold. She was probably trying to scare me. "Stupid ghost," I mumbled and went in to get started on dinner.

I set The Graveyard Book down on my bedside table and wished I could disappear from the world like Bod. The poor kid had lost his mother, too, but he was too young to understand. A tremor of longing rolled through me. No more reading tonight. I listened for Mrs. Wilson's humming. But she was gone.

The walls seemed to echo silence. It was quiet. Too quiet. Mrs. Wilson hadn't appeared when I made dinner or the entire time Dad and I were eating. And while I didn't miss her chatter, I was worried. Something wasn't right. Where was she?

The hand on my bedside clock ticked past nine. With a sigh, I settled into bed. I needed a good night's sleep so I wouldn't flunk out of Language Arts. I flipped off my bedside lamp, snuggled the duvet up to my chin, and stared at the ceiling, looking for patterns in the lumpy spackle. A star. A dinosaur. A car. The dragon Mom always saw that I thought looked like a blob with wings. I began drifting toward sleep.

Something cold prickled my nose and raised bumps along my skin. Something or someone was inside my room—right beside me.

"Mrs. Wilson?" I sat up and rubbed my eyes.

Standing right next to my bed, looking down at me, was a dark, hulking shape. Not Mrs. Wilson. Not female. And definitely not alive.

Inhale. Exhale. Inhale. Exhale. Heavy breathing whistled past an invisible moustache.

Cold tethers of terror took root in my stomach and spread outward like a splotch of blood on fresh gauze.

The presence grew more intense. The feeling of dread pressed down on me, squeezing the air and warmth and hope from my body.

My muscles tensed. Ready to flee. Or fight. Who was I kidding? I'd run, or limp, as fast as I could. I didn't want to face whoever—or whatever—was standing there. I forced a swallow and tried to ignore the dreadful entity.

An icy hand trailed over my chest, stopping right above my heart. It thumped wildly, giving away my fear.

A low moan reverberated from the thing that loomed above me. Deep and terrifying.

"Stay away from her. Stay away from my house. Stay away . . ." his voice croaked, like a strangled frog, except sinister.

I leapt from bed, tripped over a lamp cord, and pulled both it and the bedside table crashing to the floor. I screamed like a savage and bolted for the bedroom door. I threw it open and took off down the hall to Dad's room.

Dad. The room smelled of cologne and mouthwash and laundry detergent. Dad smells. Good smells. Safe smells.

I rushed into his room, heart slamming into my chest.

Dad was already up, his hair sticking up at wacky angles. "What? What's happened?"

"Nothing," I lied, trying desperately to calm down. "I—I tripped over my lamp. Bad dream." I suddenly felt foolish. Like I was six years old again and running into my parents' bedroom because of a nightmare so Mom would hold me and tell me it wasn't real. But that was the problem. Mom wasn't here anymore. And this wasn't a nightmare. It was real.

I poured myself a bowl of cereal, and Dad poured himself some coffee.

"Son, I don't mind you spending the odd night in bed with me. But neither one of us sleeps as well." Which was obvious by the extra-large cup of coffee Dad had poured and the dark circles under his eyes. "If the dreams are back I'm taking you to see the doctor. We're not letting this get out of control."

I couldn't tell Dad that Dr. Midgley couldn't help with this. Probably wouldn't even believe me. Even if he did, then I'd be re-tested and who knew what would happen. Any semblance of my old life would be utterly over. There would be no more hanging out with Jason. No more trips to Dad's room for safety. No more home. "It was just one night. It probably won't happen again."

Dad stopped stirring his coffee and looked at me. "Think you're seeing ghosts again?"

Oh, man. I didn't want to lie, but how could I tell the truth when Dad was convinced that if you didn't test as a psychic at ten, then you'd never be a psychic. "No, Dad. It was just a really bad dream."

"Want to tell me about it?"

"Not really. Why relive it, right?"

Dad took a sip of coffee. "You're sure you're all right? I can cancel my afternoon showings. I'll be here for you after school."

"Nope." I spoke almost too fast, then slowed down. "No, Dad. I'm okay. Really. I'm going to see Jason after school. I'll let you know if things get too rough."

Dad tousled my hair, obviously relieved he didn't have another Alex problem to add to his list.

I saw Dad out the door and then stuffed my lunch into my backpack. A cabinet door banged shut. I lurched forward, nearly slamming my face into the wall.

"Sorry about that," Mrs. Wilson snorted.

"Where've you been?" I demanded, surprised at how angry I felt at her for abandoning me last night. I didn't want to admit it, but I sort of liked Mrs. Wilson. She was the closest thing I actually had to a mother.

"Bit jumpy after our visitor last night," she puffed, and drifted toward the television, which she'd somehow managed to turn on and tune into a talk show—despite the sigils inscribed on the screen. I wondered if the government psychics knew that ghosts could get around some of their sigils and wards. That, or maybe they were only meant to keep away the really evil ones. Boy, did I have a lot to learn.

"Well you didn't have to leave me alone, did you?"

"Humpf . . . First you don't want to talk to me. Now you're mad I left." She sighed. "You can't blame me, Alex. That man is bad." Her New Orleans accent got thicker and her essence flickered then grew solid, in a translucent sort of way.

"Man?"

"The ghost you brought home with you." A look of worry creased her forehead. "He's bad. Bad. Bad. Bad. Killed his wife years ago. It's twisted his soul."

I stopped midbreath. The man from the house. The one who terrified the woman in the wall. He was here. "K—killed his wife?"

Mrs. Wilson turned off the TV and looked at me. "He killed her. Her own husband." Fear slithered over her words, making me cringe.

"It's all right." Mrs. Wilson's face had gone all soft and maternal. "I won't let him get you."

"But—" She'd left me. I pushed down a rising tide of panic. No doctor could help with this. Neither could Dad. If I was really a psychic, there's only one person I knew to talk to. Like it or not, I had to go straight back to Aunt Elena's after school and listen to her evidence.

CHAPTER NINE

I slammed my locker door shut, made a quick check for Billy and David, who'd been keeping their distance since the incident with the sinks in the bathroom, and then took off for the school exit.

"Alex. Wait." Jason bolted toward me. "X, stop avoiding me. I'm not gonna let you. You may be able to ditch the team, but not me. Hannah already told me everything that happened inside that house, but I wanna hear it from you. Now spill." Jason slung his backpack over one shoulder and looped his other arm through mine. "Let's go."

"Wanna walk?" I asked. I didn't feel like being cramped on a noisy bus. Especially not if Jason wanted to talk.

Together we marched out the door. My hip hurt, but I ignored it.

"First, I don't think you're a freak—"

I opened my mouth, but Jason stopped me with his oh-shut-up look. "I know you. You're probably freaking out that no one will believe you and that you'll be sent away to some psychic institution for late bloomers."

That wasn't quite what I thought, but close enough. "Okay. So maybe I'm a little freaked out. I don't want Dad to send me back to Dr. Midgley. And I definitely don't want to end up shipped off to some psychic research center halfway around the world so they can study my brain."

"You really think that would happen?"

I shrugged. "How should I know? When was the last time anyone older than ten became psychic?"

Jason held up a hand to count his fingers, then let it drop. "Um, as far as I know, never. You're right. No adults need to know."

"Except Aunt Elena and Frank," I corrected him. "They're the only ones who might have a clue about what's happening to me."

"Right. But there's no way I'm letting you do this on your own. We're brothers, X. Do you know how hard it was to know you were in that hospital and there was nothing I could do to help you? It was awful." I'd never thought about that. Yeah, I guess that would be pretty hard. "I'm with you," he grinned.

"Thanks."

Jason nodded and got that face he gets when he's thinking really hard about something. "Maybe you need to look at it like hunting."

"Look at what like hunting?" My pulse rose even thinking about the time Jason and his dad had me along on a hunting trip. I'd nearly shot my own foot off.

Jason stopped. "Just hear me out. Okay?"

"Okay," I groaned. "Shoot." I smirked at my own pun and Jason rolled his eyes.

"Ghosts are pests, right?" he asked as we walked toward the town center.

"Definitely." I shoved my hands in my pockets and tried not to think of the danger I'd felt in that house with the woman's moans.

"So think about that. First, you try to deter them." His voice rose an octave and got all quivery like he was onto something big.

"Deter them?"

Jason forged on, barely even acknowledging my question. "Sure. For rats you put down poison. They cross it, then they go crawl away somewhere to die. Obviously ghosts are already dead so you can't use poison to kill them. But if you put a salt line around your house, it might work the same way. You remember reading about salt lines last year, right?"

"Uh, not really." Leave it to Jason to remember the bits I'd forgotten. I'd focused on sigils and decided to let the town psychics do the rest. At home, Mom had always handled the salt. My stomach flip-flopped at the thought of Mom. I missed her so much, and wondered if Dad had been putting salt around the house. If not, maybe that's how they were getting in?

"Now, take it a step further. If you get an aggressive ghost, then you need to become the hunter. The ghosts are your prey. So you need traps and weapons, right? Lures."

"Why in Solomon's name would I want lures? I'm trying to keep them away from me."

"I know—I know. But if you know one of them is going to show up anyway, why not lure them to the spot you want them to appear in? Maybe have a trap ready and—" Jason clapped his hands shut. "Snap. You got one. Then it won't bother you anymore." He smiled like he'd come up with the cleverest plan on the planet.

"It's a good idea, but isn't that what the psychics at OPI are supposed to do?"

"I guess. Only time I've ever met one was when they gave us that presentation in fifth grade on ghost hunting . . . but if you want them to stop bothering you, then maybe your best defense is to start thinking like a ghost-hunting psychic."

Darn it. I knew Jason was onto something, and I had a sinking feeling he was right.

We rounded the corner to Decatur Street with its colorful balconied buildings shoulder to shoulder, and I led the way to Elena's Paranormal Investigation Services. An open sign hung in the window.

I reached for the door and Jason stopped. "Whoa." He traced a finger along a faint, but glimmering sigil inscribed on the door. "You ever seen a seal like this?"

What seal? I hadn't noticed a seal on her front door before—except the usual Third Pentacle of Jupiter, which everyone had. I looked closer. Complex lines and markings curved around one another, forming what

I guessed was some sort of advanced protective sigil. I shivered. "I have no idea. But let's see if she's here and find out what she and Frank had actually caught on their equipment."

Nerves coursed through me and I let the door to Aunt Elena's office slam a little harder than I should, sending its tinkling chimes into a twirling vortex of trills.

Hannah's voice drifted over the gentle thrum of the ceiling fan. Great. Just what I needed. I'd been avoiding her all day at school. Coming clean with Jason had been enough for one day. The last thing I needed was her harassing me about seeing ghosts.

I trudged to the back of the store, Jason following close behind.

Aunt Elena sat hunched forward in her office chair, Frank sat beside her, both looking at several monitors inscribed with some weird seals we never learned in elementary school. Hannah peered over their shoulders. When they heard me, they all looked up.

Hannah's lips quirked into a smile. "I knew you'd come."

"I'm glad you came to your senses." Elena extended her hand toward Jason. "I assume you're the infamous friend Jason I've heard about over the years."

Jason shook her hand and gave her one of his best grins. "I don't know about infamous, but it's lovely to meet you."

Oh. My. Gosh. Hannah giggled. She actually giggled, her pale cheeks flaring pink. Jason was turning on the charm here? With her?

Aunt Elena gestured to a couple of empty chairs nearby, which we promptly dragged over to the monitor. "Alex, Frank thinks you're sensing a lot more than you let on."

Frank looked at me with an expression that would suit a hungry wolf.

"Uh," was all I could manage before I sat down.

"Have a look at this." Aunt Elena motioned to the screen.

Jason eyed the spiky reading on the monitor, then glanced at a still image of me from the video. "I have no idea what we're looking at, but cool."

I took a deep breath and looked at the frozen video image. My face was pale. And, yeah, I did look sort of freaked out.

Aunt Elena clicked a few buttons and the video came to life. "Our EMF readings were off the charts when you were so agitated."

"Agitated? He totally freaked," Hannah snorted, her eyes giddy.

"And you wonder why he wouldn't talk to you all day?" Elena wedged herself between us, almost making me want to hug her.

"Okay. Here we are." Aunt Elena pushed another button. The screen went dark; hissing filled the silence. Then we heard something. Breathing.

I wasn't sure if it was my breath or that creepy man-ghost. Then I spoke.

"Can you hear that?" Me, totally annoyed and a little freaked out.

"Hear what?" Hannah's voice. Then my squinting face, hand shielding my eyes, filled the frame.

"Fast-forward it, Aunt Elena. Get to the good part," Hannah huffed.

Good part? How could any of this have a good part?

Aunt Elena moved her mouse and clicked. "Here's the footage from when Hannah came back with me and Frank. There. Listen." She tilted her head toward the screen.

My back was to the camera, my hand outstretched, fingers grazing the wall. Then came a high-pitched voice. Thin and frail and frightened. "Please . . . please . . ." Tears choked her voice and garbled her words, but there it was. Caught on tape.

I stood frozen in the video, my breathing harsh and tight. The woman's voice came back. "Oh, please. I beg you . . . He's coming."

I screamed. The camera panned over the floor, the wall, the ceiling.

"Turn it off." I swallowed, feeling the blood drain from my face.

A scuffle and the screen went dark. Only Hannah's voice. "The readings are off the charts."

"Turn it off." I wanted to break something. Make it all go away. But I couldn't. It was real. All of it. And now I had proof. I turned away from Jason, trying not to cry in front of my best friend.

"Hannah, please flip the store sign to Closed."

"Now? But it's only four o'clock."

"Do it now," Frank growled at her, not taking his eyes off me.

Hannah silently obeyed.

Aunt Elena touched my arm. "Alex, Hannah told me that you've been seeing and hearing spirits since your mother died. She told me you're worried that no one will believe you because you tested as an Untouched." She tapped her finger lightly against her lips, then pointed to the screen. "But every time you responded in the video, it was in reaction to one of the voices on the tape. And our EMF readings correspond with it. Frank sensed it, too, and his infrared picked up cold spots behind the wall. So, whether you want to admit it or not, this is proof. You are psychic."

"That is so cool." Hannah's enthusiasm was annoying as she bounced toward us from the storefront like nothing on the planet could possibly scare her.

"No," I said, studying the faded design on the carpet. "It's not."

"So you admit it, then?" Hannah's face glowed with triumph.

I looked from her to Aunt Elena to Frank to Jason. Would they really believe me? Would they help me? Or would they tell Dad and have me sent away?

Frank's dark eyes were serious, and for the first time I noticed a tattoo in the hollow of his throat—a symbol, one of Solomon's Seals, but not the Third Pentacle of Jupiter. Inside the circle was a pointing hand inscribed with Hebrew. If I remembered correctly, it was rare and very powerful: the Fourth Pentacle of the Moon. A sigil meant to protect the body and soul from all evil.

Frank's eyes met mine and he gestured to a nearby chair. "We need to talk. Now."

There was no way I was going to make it home for dinner. So I called Dad and told him I wanted to hang out with Hannah and Jason, which Dad was totally cool with. Thankfully. We ate Chinese food from little paper cartons while I told Elena and Frank everything. About the accident. About my broken hip and leg. About the surgery. About seeing Mom in the hospital. About how Dad and the psychiatrists thought I was seeing things as some sort of post-traumatic psychosis.

"And I thought things were getting better." I stared at my scuffed-up Nikes. The ones I wouldn't toss out even though my feet were starting to press so hard against the tips my toes hurt. Mom had bought them for me—a week before the accident—and I wasn't going to lose them, too. "When I first got home I didn't see a thing. I figured, you know—" I dug a toe into the carpet. "I figured I was healing."

"But there's nothing wrong with you." Frank crossed his arms over his chest, the tattoo of the gargoyle on his forearm staring at me. "In fact, we need more people like you. The Problem isn't going to go away on its own."

Aunt Elena's face lit up. "You could take him on—"

"I'm retired. I'm not taking on another apprentice, Elena," Frank growled.

There was more than anger in his growl, there was sadness, too. But I didn't care. I was relieved. I was damaged and I didn't want to be an apprentice or a psychic. "I'll never fully heal—ever. Not my hip, and obviously not my mind."

"You're cool, X." Jason thumped my shoulder and gave me an awkward nod. Oh, Jason. Thank God for you. I think I could've grown horns out of my head and he'd still be there for me.

"Tell us what else you've seen." Aunt Elena gave me an encouraging nod.

"Well, after those first few days home, I saw Mrs. Wilson. And since then . . ." I told them about the janitor and about what I'd seen and felt at the haunted house. About the evil spirit in my bedroom.

"Ghosts don't usually follow people from the place they're attached to . . ." Aunt Elena tapped a finger against the table, stood, and went to a bookshelf. She selected a fat volume and skimmed through the pages. "Unless," she said, scanning the text.

"Unless what?" Hannah leapt up and went to read over our aunt's shoulder.

"Unless the ghost is particularly strong," Frank finished for her and looked straight at me. "Or unless the haunted has an object belonging to the deceased. It's easier for them to attach to someone if that person has something that belonged to him."

Jason gave me one of his You didn't, did you? looks.

Elena glanced over at me. "Did you take anything from the house?"

I shook my head, then stopped. I thought back to the living room. To the basement door. "The basement door," I sputtered. "It was locked. I put the key in my pocket."

"What on God's green earth were you thinking?" Frank bellowed. Hands slamming the table, he nearly startled me out of my chair, making me feel like a complete idiot.

Elena grabbed me by the shoulders. "Where is it now? Do you have it?"

"It's—it's at home. On my bedside table."

Jason mouthed the word lure.

I wanted to tell him to shut up, but I was too freaked out.

Elena looked at the clock. "It's too late tonight, but I'll get in touch with Mr. Barrett and see if we can go back tomorrow."

"No way. I'm not going back in there," my voice rose, threatening to crack.

"If you want that spirit to leave you alone, then we have to return the key. And we certainly can't leave that poor woman trapped down there." Frank began pacing.

Hannah's face got really pale and Jason shuffled from one foot to another like he was going to pee his pants.

"I'll go with you," Hannah whispered. And for a moment I was actually glad she was there—sort of.

"Yeah, me, too." Jason stood beside her, but didn't sound convinced. Still, I knew where I went, he'd follow. We always had each other's backs.

Elena selected another text. The subtitle said something about helping earthbound spirits cross over. I shivered. I so didn't want to do this.

"I've helped spirits cross into the light before, Alex. Not as often as Frank, but this should help, don't you think?" She showed the book to Frank, who read the title and nodded.

She handed me the book and smiled. A smile that reminded me too much of Mom when she understood that I was afraid but was going to make me do something I didn't want anyway. "You wouldn't want to be killed and left trapped in a basement wall, would you?"

A shiver crawled over my arms. "No," I whispered. "Of course not."

"Right," she said, with a hand on my shoulder. "Then we can't leave her there. We must help her. You must help her."

"Why does it have to be me?" I winced at the whine in my voice, but I couldn't help it. The last place I wanted to be was where some lady had been killed. Especially when the killer still lurked there and knew where I lived.

"Because she reached out to you," Frank said, crouching in front of me, his Fourth Pentacle of the Moon tattoo peeking out from beneath his collar. For once his voice was soft, almost kind. "Because you have a gift that many psychics and paranormal investigators only dream of having. And because you have the power to send her murderous husband away from this world and set his wife free."

"Jason, Hannah, come with me," said Aunt Elena, who led them toward the storeroom. "We're going to get a few things together for Alex."

Hannah opened her mouth to protest, but a scowl from Frank sent her scurrying.

Frank took an empty chair beside me. "Look, Alex. I know what it's like to lose your friends because you're different. When I tested as a psychic, my whole life changed. Then, when I was named a Class A Psychic, my life changed again." He rolled up his sleeves revealing more tattoos on his upper arm. He pointed at a small Seal of Solomon there. "Do you know this one?"

"Um . . . it's a Third Pentacle of Saturn?" I guessed. I hadn't paid as much attention in my elementary warding as I should.

"You're right, but you can't be unsure about your seals. You have to know them. I got this when I was confirmed a Class A Psychic. The rest I've acquired over the years." He ran his fingers over the various seals and symbols on his arms. "Some are for protection . . . others—others are reminders." He stared at me hard. "You can't escape who you are. You have to embrace it. You'll keep your true friends and make new ones. Friends that are like you. Friends who understand."

I didn't want new friends, and I didn't want to be different. I wanted to be the same old Alex who'd won ghostball championships. The same old Alex who lived with his mom and dad and didn't see ghosts. I wanted to be Untouched.

Frank rubbed the back of his neck. "I don't want another apprentice, but I also won't leave you alone to deal with this. I'll do some reading tonight. Tomorrow we'll go to the house and see what we can do to rid you of your troublesome spirit and bring peace back to the place."

I barely nodded and tucked the book Aunt Elena had given me into my backpack. I supposed I didn't have a choice.

Aunt Elena bustled back into the room holding a glass bottle; Hannah and Jason followed her, both lugging large bags of salt. "This is holy water from the Jordan River," she said, and handed me the bottle.

Holy water. Great. I hadn't been to church in months. Not since before Mom died. But I remembered enough from Sunday school and warding class to know what that meant.

"The Jordan River's where Jesus was baptized by John the Baptist," Hannah offered, plopping her bag on the ground beside Jason's.

"I know that," I snapped without meaning to.

"Right," said Elena, her face serious. "If that man—yes, Alex, he is only a man, even if he's in spirit form—gives you any more trouble, sprinkle him with the holy water."

Frank didn't look convinced, but I took the bottle anyway. I needed all the help I could get.

Elena ignored Frank's scowl and kept talking. "It won't drive him away completely, but it should be enough to keep him away until we can return the key, free his wife, and make him go to the other side."

I gripped the bottle in my sweaty palm and hoped Elena was right. There was no way I would sleep in my room again if that monster was still in it.

Susan McCauley

Chapter Ten

I snuggled under my duvet and started reading. If only I had special talents like Bod in The Graveyard Book. Maybe if I'd actually grown up seeing ghosts like Bod or any normal psychic, then I wouldn't be so freaked out right now. A freaked-out freak. So much for being the most popular ghostball player at school. I scowled at Mrs. Wilson's round bottom, which sat plunked on the edge of my bed. She hadn't said a word, but kept bouncing. Bouncing. Bouncing. It was driving me crazy.

"Would you please stop," I snapped. "I told you we've got holy water. If he comes back, I'll throw it on him." I sounded way braver than I felt. Who was I to try and comfort a ghost, anyway? I set the book on the bedside table, picked up the three-ounce vial of holy water, and studied it. Would it actually do any good?

"What could have happened to the key?" It was the six hundredth time Mrs. Wilson had asked the question.

"I told you. I. Don't. Know." I rummaged around my bedside table again. "It was there last night. Now it's gone."

"And you've checked the floor? Under the bed?"

"You know I have. And if you ask me one more time, I'll dump the holy water on you," I growled, feeling instantly guilty I'd said something so nasty.

But the squeaking bounce of my bed stopped immediately, and Mrs. Wilson sat frozen on the edge . . . her eyes superglued to the door.

The handle twitched and began to slowly turn.

My chest grew tight and I gripped the glass vial, hard—ready to spray the nasty spirit.

The handle turned all the way.

I put my thumb just below the plastic lid and prepared to pop the top.

The door creaked open; Mrs. Wilson let out a high-pitched shriek and tore out of the room.

The door swung open.

Dad.

I let the bottle of holy water dip beneath the covers. If I wasn't so scared, I would have laughed at Mrs. Wilson who had shot through the bedroom wall in a blur.

Dad came in and sat on my bedside, his well-trained eyes avoiding the family picture with Mom that I kept on my dresser—the only picture of her up anywhere in the house. Maybe that's why Dad barely ever came in here. "I thought I saw your light on. What are you still doing up?"

I dropped the bottle of holy water under the sheets, reached over, and grabbed my book. "Reading."

"The Graveyard Book?" Dad squinted at the cover.

"It's for Language Arts. It's on the required reading list." I flipped it open.

"Humpf." Dad didn't look impressed. "How is it?"

"Pretty good." I didn't say that I wished I knew Bod and his graveyard full of ghosts. Maybe then I'd actually know how to handle them better.

Dad took the book and read the back cover. "I'm not sure you should be reading about ghosts right now. It might make your nightmares worse."

Not this again. "It's fiction, Dad."

He set the book on the nightstand. "Well if it gets too much for you or you start having those nightmares again, let me know. Dr. Midgley is only a phone call away. I'm sure he'll be glad to write a letter to the teacher . . ."

I'll bet he would. Dr. Midgley had been the one who'd convinced Dad that no one could see ghosts or be psychic if they didn't already have the abilities by age ten—something about brain development—and that I was really suffering from post-traumatic stress disorder. If he wrote a note, then all of the teachers at Rey would think I was wacko. "No thanks. I mean, I'm fine. Really. It's just a book."

"Okay . . ." Dad gave me a stiff kiss on the forehead. Not something he usually did. "Maybe just try to read it during the day. Not right before you go to sleep."

"Don't worry, Dad." The holy water rolled against my leg as if to remind me that not worrying was definitely not going to happen. "I'll be fine," I lied.

Dad stood up and flicked off the bedside lamp. "All right, then. Have a good night's sleep."

I lay back, whispered a prayer as I touched Mom's amulet, then gripped the holy water in my hand and closed my eyes.

Thunder rumbled, leaves thrashed, and rain slapped against my bedroom window, ripping me away from the comfort of sleep. My eyes snapped open and darted around the shadows of my room. White walls. The alarm clock, glowing pale green. My picture with Mom.

A scratching rustle made me sit up on my elbows and look toward the window. My sigils were still intact. Good.

Skretch.

It must be a tree branch.

Skretch.

Whatever it was, it wasn't at the window. I sat up a little taller and looked around the room. Maybe a squirrel had gotten inside looking for shelter.

Skretch.

The sound of claws against the floorboards crept right up next to me. I tossed back the covers, ready to bolt. But something cold shoved me back in bed so hard the air left my lungs in a whoosh. I gasped, struggling for breath. Then the pressure started, like an elephant sitting on my chest.

The pressure was so intense I could barely breathe. I opened my mouth to call out. For Mrs. Wilson. For Dad. For anybody . . . but only a small whoosh of air escaped and Mom's Nazar Boncuğu amulet slid uselessly over my shoulder. So much for it keeping evil away. If I didn't do something, and soon, I'd black out. I'd die.

And I didn't want to die.

I'd survived the accident for some reason. I had to survive this. I fumbled under the sheets, fingers groping for the holy water I must've dropped while I was sleeping.

The bed shook, rattling itself against the wall, then began to rise. A low moan of cold air hissed out of the entity's mouth, inches from my face.

If I could scream, I'd do it now. I didn't care if Dad thought I was crazy. There was a real evil presence in my room. Right on top of me. And if I didn't find the holy water, this ghost was going to kill me.

Nails tearing over the sheets, I searched the spaces between the pillows. A cool glass bottle rolled against my arm. I hooked the bottle in the crook of my left arm, then wiggled my right hand across the top of my chest. I couldn't quite reach it.

The entity laughed. The same cold, dark laugh I'd heard when I found the desperate woman calling through the basement wall.

I shimmied my left arm up, right hand reaching down. My fingers grazed the plastic cap. Almost.

There. Got it. I flipped the lid off with my right thumb, tore my hand loose from the covers, and threw the contents of the entire bottle on the dark mass.

A scream more horrific than the screeching of car metal clashing filled the room. The weight immediately lifted from me and a sharp pain jolted my wrist, knocking the empty bottle from my hand. A roar of anger ripped through my bedroom, blowing the books from their shelves, and finally exploding through the bedroom window.

Glass rained down on the carpet like shredded glitter.

I cupped my throbbing wrist and sat totally still. Waiting. Watching. Wondering if he was gone.

Silence except for the soft patter of rain and rustle of leaves.

There was no way . . . no way . . . I'd be able to explain any of this to Dad.

Susan McCauley

Chapter Eleven

T hankfully, Dad was a deep sleeper. And the rain and thunder and wind had certainly helped. Still, I had no idea how he hadn't heard the bed rattling, or the books flying off their shelves, or my bedroom window exploding. But he hadn't.

At least I didn't have to go to school today. Dad had bought my story that a branch had come crashing through my window in the storm and that I'd slept terribly through the thunder.

I'd already put all the books back on the shelves by the time Dad appeared to inspect the damage. He'd called in late to work and taped heavy-duty trash bags over the broken window. I didn't care so long as the bugs and rain and that evil ghost didn't get in. But Dad was on a mission to get the window fixed and left the house with his cell phone glued to his ear.

"My son won't be able to sleep in there without a window . . . Yes, this afternoon should work—" The front door banged closed and I watched Dad climb into the minivan he'd purchased after the accident. "A five-star safety rating and plenty of room to tote clients and kids," he'd said. Never mind that I had no intention of playing ghostball or being toted around ever again.

I grabbed my backpack, an apple for breakfast, and left the house. I needed answers. And I headed straight for the one place I knew I could find them

The sign for Aunt Elena's office flapped back and forth in the early autumn breeze. The Closed sign hung crooked in the window. I tried the handle anyway. Locked. I rapped on the glass door, hoping Aunt Elena was there. I didn't want to discuss this at her house in front of Hannah or Aunt Trudy.

"Alex?" A rustle of skirts and jingle of keys fluttered up behind me. "Why aren't you in school? It's nearly ten o'clock."

"Dad knows I'm not in school," I said, wondering why I felt the need to explain myself, but glad she was here. I thought my aunt was a bit crazy. Dad had always called her "eccentric." Maybe she was, but she was also smart. A true PI.

She stepped past me and unlocked the front door, eyeing my bandaged wrist. "Never mind school. Come in and tell me what happened."

After flipping on an electric, sigil-covered kettle and preparing two cups of chamomile tea, Elena sat me down and stared. "Talk."

So I did. I told her about having trouble falling asleep and the storm and the scratching noise. "Then something tossed me back on the bed and it felt like all of the air was being squeezed out of my lungs."

Aunt Elena didn't say a word while I spoke, but her brows drew together. "Well," she finally said. "It sounds like you've attracted a malevolent spirit."

"You mean like the ones the federal psychics come in to take care of?" A lump like a slug slid down my throat, cold and wet.

"I'm not sure." Aunt Elena stood up and skimmed her fingers over the titles on her bookshelf. "Start with this." She thrust a book into my hands: How to Clear Your Home of Ghosts and Spirits.

Great. "Why do I have to do it? Why not Frank?"

"Frank? Frank had an issue with his last apprentice." Aunt Elena pressed her lips together like she wanted to say more, but wouldn't. "Besides, like Frank said, you have to do it because you are psychic and because the spirit followed you home."

"Isn't there anyone else?" I groaned.

"The last I heard you were totally against telling any adult, except me and Frank, about your gift. Especially not your dad. Or, you could file a claim with the feds and wait six to twelve months for OPI to respond."

"Six months to a year?" I knew they were slow, but there's no way I could live with a murderous spirit hunting me down every night for a year.

"It's their backlog that keeps PIs like me in business." Her eyes gleamed. "And with your gift, Alex, you can do wonderful things."

A gift? Being psychic wasn't a gift. It was a curse. Ugh. Maybe Aunt Elena wanted me to be psychic because it would be good for business. Her business. But it wasn't good for me. I pulled away from her, wondering how much she really cared about me.

She must have noticed my expression, because she immediately softened. "I know it's hard, Alex. But you can do it. I believe in you." She tapped her fingers together for a moment. "Did you bring the key?"

I scratched a tickle at the base of my skull. "I—I can't find it."

"And you've looked everywhere?"

"Yeah." My voice cracked. "It's not where I put it. And it's not under my bed. Even Mrs. Wilson looked. It's gone."

Aunt Elena went to a wooden cabinet and removed a large bag of salt followed by another bottle of holy water and set them on the table in front of me. "Until you're ready to tell your father, I'll help you as much as I can."

"Um, that will be never."

She frowned at me like a kid who'd been caught stealing candy from the cupboard before Halloween, but I wasn't going to budge. "You may not have a choice, Alex. Now, take these with you. Spread the salt around the edges of your room and house. Don't forget the windows. Make sure the salt lines aren't broken. This should help." She handed me another bottle of holy water. "And keep this with you—just in case."

"And what are you going to do?"

"I'm going to arrange for us to pay a visit to Mr. Graves."

Mr. Graves? I didn't like the sound of that.

The window repairman had fixed my window, and I checked my Spellguard. It was already three o'clock, which meant I had to hurry and salt the house before Jason or Hannah arrived to find out why I wasn't at school.

I glanced at the book Aunt Elena had given me, then back at Dad's computer—the only computer in the house. The government permitted one computer per household. One television. One of anything that was powered with electricity. Electric machines, especially computers, had caused a lot of trouble in the early days after they were invented. But scientists had argued that scientific and technological progress should not be stopped due to the spirit attacks and hauntings we'd encountered since the Great Unleashing of 1900. And they had worked right along with some of the best government psychics to stop spirit activity in their machines. Apparently, entities like to travel through electric lines and computers. So, the OPI created a Paranormal Cybersecurity Squad to stop computer-related hauntings. And all electronics were sold with warded wires and nearly invisible Solomon's Seals etched into the screens.

Still, I triple-checked the seals before switching it on; then I did what most normal twelve-year-olds do when using a computer—an Internet search.

I typed malevolent spirit, and prayed one wouldn't come shooting out at me through the screen.

A definition popped up. Good. Maybe I was on the right track. I read the screen.

A malevolent spirit is the soul of a human being who had ill intentions while living. Since spirits retain the same personalities they had while alive, these spirits can be angry, troublesome, and plain nasty.

That sounded like my ghost all right. If he really did kill the woman in the basement, then he might try to do the same thing to me.

Next I clicked on a link for town psychics and skimmed a list of ways to rid a place of dark and evil spirits.

1. Holy water

2. Sea salt

3. Candles

4. Incense (especially sage)

5. Prayer

6. Feng shui

Those were listed as the top six; I skipped the legendary uses of garlic and painting the door red. Those were definitely things Dad would notice. I'd better use the holy water and salt like I'd learned in elementary warding.

I waited until after the repairman had replaced the window to haul Elena's bag of salt out from where I'd hidden it under my bed. I grabbed a clean bucket and a Pyrex measuring cup from the kitchen, when someone pounded on my back door.

Startled, I dropped the bucket, shoved it under the kitchen table, and went to the door.

"Who is it?" I called through the haze of window sheers that obscured my view.

"It's me. Jason. Hurry up and let me in."

I unlocked the door with a relieved sigh. "I'm glad it's you."

Jason eyed the Pyrex measuring cup on the counter and sniffed. "Where were you today and what are you up to?"

Quickly, I told him about the attack last night and how Aunt Elena had instructed me to salt the house. Without question, Jason helped me load the bucket and Pyrex measuring cup with salt and we began spreading.

We put a thick layer around the periphery of the house's interior, carefully lining every doorway and window, and sprinkling it around the perimeter of each room.

My room was last, and I insisted we put an extra-large amount there, adding even more around my bed. That should do it. My bed was like an island surrounded by a sea of salt.

Jason surveyed our work. "I don't know, X. There is a lot of salt here. Your dad might notice."

"Nah. As long as he doesn't put his reading glasses on and look at the floor, I think I'll be okay." I hoped.

"What you need," said Jason, who stood looking around my room, "is a trap."

"A trap?"

Jason went over to my dresser and started digging through my drawers where I'd always kept my ghostball uniforms and supplies. "Sure. You brought the ghost home with a lure—the key."

"Which is missing," I snarled, still annoyed I couldn't find it.

Jason picked up an old ghostball, letting my attitude roll off him. "That doesn't matter. Even if it's gone, he's still coming back. So, you're the lure now. And if there's one thing I know about hunting, you don't want to use a lure without a trap." He tossed the ghostball to me with a grin.

I looked at the ghostball in my hands, then at Jason. "I think I know what you have in mind."

Together we dove for the ghostball gear I'd boxed up after the accident.

I ripped open a box and hefted out a new, unprimed ghostball still in its package.

"Cool." Jason took the ball from me. "I'm glad you have one that's not primed."

Suddenly I didn't feel so sure. Usually when you got a new ghostball, it came with sigils, but no entity. The State Ghostball referees were the ones to put in a poltergeist and make sure the sigils were sound and the ball worked properly. "It's empty, but how are we going to prime it to catch a ghost?"

Jason pulled a book entitled Ghost Traps and Tricks out of his backpack. "You're not the only one doing some reading. Here." He handed me the book. "You've always been better with wards and sigils, so you can do it. I'll hold the ball."

I flipped open the book to an earmarked page: lure and trapping sigils. Right. I read them over and picked out the ones I thought would work best for pulling a ghost into the ball, then I grabbed a small can of black iron paint I hadn't used since fifth grade when I'd had my sigil class and got to work on the ball.

By the time we were done, Dad was home. And I prayed tonight wouldn't be as bad as the last.

Mrs. Wilson was still scarce. Maybe it was the salt. Maybe it was her fear. Either way, I couldn't blame her. I carefully checked the line of salt around my room and the trap Jason and I had prepared. Nothing had been disturbed. Good. Next I took the new bottle of holy water from my jeans pocket and tucked it into the waistband of my boxer shorts. Then I climbed into bed, ready for battle. And, after what felt like hours, I drifted into a restless sleep.

My eyes shot open, my head tilted uncomfortably sideways. I was staring straight at the ghostly, glowing digits of my alarm clock: 2:00 a.m.

A huge thud banged against my bedroom window followed by the rattle, rattle, rattle of the glass in its panes.

I sat up, hugging my knees to my chest.

Thud. Rattle. Rattle. Rattle.

I didn't feel cold. Not even the chill I got when Mrs. Wilson was around.

Thud. Rattle. Rattle. Rattle.

I flipped on my bedside lamp, and looked over to my partly drawn drapes.

Thud. Rattle. Rattle. Rattle.

The shape of a fist beat against the window, then shook it. Someone was trying to get in.

I tried to swallow the vise-like grip that now clenched my throat, and climbed out of bed. I checked the salt line. It was unbroken. The ghostball sat still, its sigils not glowing. I wouldn't need it unless the spirit got inside.

The windowpane shook with so much force the glass bulged. I took another step closer. Maybe if the thing outside couldn't see inside it would go away.

I reached out and grabbed the curtains to pull them tight, and stopped dead. There. Staring straight at me through my locked second-story bedroom window was the ghost. The man was mostly translucent, but his eyes flashed red, then faded to a putrid brown, and his lips curled with hatred.

Heart thundering, I forced the curtains shut.

The man howled, more like some wild creature than a human, and the window exploded inward, showering me with glass.

Pain seared my face and arms as the glass made tiny slices in my skin. I leapt into bed, pulled the duvet snuggly over my head to protect myself from any more flying glass, grabbed the holy water, and prayed the salt lines held.

The screaming went on and on. More windows rattled. But he couldn't come inside. The howl lasted for what seemed like hours before it finally died away—the thumping and rattling with it.

Dad trembled with fury as he swept up a pile of shredded glass. "How do you explain this? Another branch?"

I looked anywhere but at Dad. What could I say when he didn't want to hear the truth?

"There wasn't a storm last night, Alex." He swept up another pile. "You're doing this, aren't you?" Dad stood up and dumped the final shards of glass into the extra-thick yard bag he'd brought up from the garage. "I'm spending too much time at work and you're trying to get my attention. I'm calling Dr. Midgley."

Dad bent down to pick up a large sliver he'd missed, then stopped. He reached for something under the bed.

My stomach fell into my toes and I fought the urge to bolt. Please let it only be the ghostball.

Dad got on his hands and knees, reached under the bed, and lifted up the bottle of holy water that must've slipped out of my underwear. "What. Is. This?" He read the bottle and a strange, totally freaked-out look took over his face. "Holy water. Where did you get holy water?"

I opened my mouth. Closed it.

Dad tossed it on the bed. "Never mind. Don't answer that. This has got to stop."

"You're right, Dad. It does have to stop. And I'm trying to—"

Dad held up his hand. "Just go to school, Alex. We'll discuss it later. You're late."

As soon as Dad left the room, I grabbed the holy water and shoved it in my pocket. Then I grabbed my extra-large backpack, shoved my ghostball trap inside, and headed for school.

Chapter Twelve

Mr. Daniels, our math teacher, droned on about equations. Problems I could do in my sleep. And if I had one more sleepless night I would be doing them in my sleep. I needed to meet up with Jason and Hannah immediately after school. I needed to find that key and get it back to that house so that nasty ghost would go away.

After what felt like an eternity, the bell rang for lunch. I headed straight to the bathroom. Maybe some cold water on the face would help wake me up. Hannah and Jason didn't need to know how little I'd been sleeping.

"Hey." Billy's voice echoed off the tiled walls and linoleum floor.

I groaned. I should have gone straight to lunch. I hadn't even heard Billy and David come in.

"You may not want to play on the team anymore, but you don't have to be rude." Billy shouldered past me and I stumbled against the edge of the sink. Yep. That'll leave a bruise.

So much for not burning bridges.

Then a deep growl sounded from one of the stalls.

Mr. Thomas, the shot-up janitor, hovered a few feet away. But his bloodshot eyes were open in wide-eyed terror. "Best get out of here, son. And quick."

A shadowy figure shot through the white tile walls, blotting out the light like an eclipse.

One by one the hot-water faucets turned on. The mirrors began to fog and the lights shook in their sockets.

"Oh, crap." David backed away staring at me. "He's doing it, isn't he?"

The lights shook more violently and the mirrors trembled. The sickening cold feeling wrapped its arms around me and squeezed. He couldn't get me at home, but he could get me here. Sure we had sigils at school, but the feds only repainted them at the start of each term—if we were lucky and they weren't shorthanded.

The mirrors cracked. Not fast, but slow. I watched the fractures as they wove their way through the glass.

Ignoring my old teammates, Mr. Thomas wedged himself between me and the splintering glass. "Duck, son. Now."

I ducked. Actually, I dove straight under the sink and covered my head with my already bandaged arms.

"Freak," David yelled, backing toward the bathroom door.

The mirrors exploded along with the most terrifying moan I'd ever heard.

Billy and David ran shrieking from the bathroom as the glass rained down around me. A shard sliced my battered arms, and cold, inhuman hands gripped my neck.

I tried to scream, but all that came out was a strangled groan.

"Keep—away," the voice snarled.

I shoved my hand deep into my jeans pocket and grabbed the bottle of holy water.

The invisible fingers squeezed harder. It took everything I had not to clutch at the frigid fingers and try to yank them from my neck. I pulled out the bottle and tried to flip off the plastic lid.

It slipped from my grasp and clattered to the floor.

The lights flickered out, plunging the room into icy darkness. Heavy breathing hissed in my ear and the ghost tightened his grip, making my heart pulse in my neck.

"I'll have none of that done to one of my students," Mr. Thomas growled, his voice fierce and protective.

The grip around my neck loosened and the malevolent spirit swung to stare at Mr. Thomas.

His face paled, but he stood his ground. "Get outta here, Alex. Go now."

I scooted backward toward the bathroom door. Ghosts couldn't kill each other, could they? They were already dead.

The evil spirit screamed and lunged itself at Mr. Thomas. "You shouldn't have interfered."

The two entities clawed at each other, hissing and screaming and wailing until I thought my eardrums would burst. Mr. Thomas hit the floor. "Go now, son. Save yourself."

The dark spirit opened his mouth like a cavern and bit deeply into the janitor's ghostly flesh. Mr. Thomas howled in agony, but looked at me with pleading eyes. "Run."

I ran.

The bathroom door slammed shut behind me and I scurried into the hall. I needed to see Aunt Elena. I needed to talk to Frank. I needed to stop this evil entity from causing any more harm.

Heels pressed against the metal legs of the chair, I tapped my feet against the linoleum floor, nursed the claw marks on my neck with a damp paper towel, and waited. Waited for Principal Harper. Waited for Dad. Ugh.

Billy and David were in the principal's office now. And he wasn't happy. If I hadn't been in trouble, I'd have laughed at the way Billy's voice squeaked. We'd been teammates, true, but he and David had never been my favorite people.

"It was him. I swear it," David whined. "He got all mad and started smashing mirrors . . ."

What a liar. I squirmed in my seat. I could barely stand to sit here and listen, but I wasn't fixing to go barging into the principal's office making more trouble. Principal Harper said something, but I couldn't make out what. Whatever it was, it wasn't good.

There was a scooting of chairs and a scuffle of feet and the door creaked open. Billy and David edged out, away from me. I gave them a leering scowl. If they thought I was actually causing the supernatural freak show, then good. I'd use it to scare them away. They'd never bother me about playing ghostball or not being polite again.

"Alex." Principal Harper opened the door to his office wider. "Please come in."

I pulled the bloodied tissue from my neck, crumpled it, and tossed it in the trash.

"Did Billy do that to you?" Principal Harper closed the door and examined the scratch marks on my neck before looking down at the bandages on my arms.

"No, sir."

"Then how did it happen?"

"I'm—I'm not sure," I lied.

"Okay, then sit down and tell me exactly what did happen."

I sat on the well-worn brown sofa that took up most of the wall and tried to figure out how to get out of this. "Um . . . Well, David and Billy followed me into the bathroom. They started giving me a hard time about not rejoining the team, and then . . ." What could I say? That an evil ghost showed up, busted out the mirrors, and tried to strangle me? Never mind that the school's dead janitor had come to save me? I'd be hauled off to be tested as the first ever kid to become psychic at age twelve, and would never see my father or Jason again. "Things started to happen. Billy pushed past me and I hit the edge of the sink. Then I ducked when I heard the glass cracking."

"So, Billy pushed you?"

"Sort of."

"And David?"

I shook my head. "He was just standing there."

"Then what made the glass break?"

"I'm not sure. I didn't see—"

Three heavy raps interrupted the interrogation.

"Come in," Principal Harper huffed.

The door swung open. Dad. I swear he looks a foot taller when he's angry.

"Principal Harper."

"Mr. Lenard." Principal Harper stood and shook Dad's hand. They both sat and I swallowed the ostrich egg of fear lodged in my throat.

"Alex was just telling me what happened. About the scratches on his neck."

Dad leaned forward and took a closer look. "Scratches?" His eyes widened. "And bruises. Are they bullying you, son?"

I saw fear and relief and hope swirling in Dad's face. If only it were that easy.

But I couldn't full-out lie. "They're trying to get me to rejoin the team, but no. They're not bullying me. They ran off when the mirrors broke."

"You broke mirrors?" Dad's voice rose an octave.

"No," I moaned. "I don't know how they broke." So, I started over and retold Dad what I'd told Principal Harper.

"And you didn't see what broke the glass?" Skepticism dripped from Dad's voice. Principal Harper didn't look convinced either. After the windows breaking in my room two days in a row, this didn't look good. I needed to get outta here and over to Aunt Elena's.

"Did you do it?" Principal Harper asked what Dad was thinking. "You can tell us, Alex. Was it an accident because you were afraid?"

"No." I cracked my knuckles and hoped they believed me.

"And what about the marks on your neck?" Dad knew I was keeping something from them; I heard that edge in his voice.

I shrugged. I didn't want to lie anymore and he didn't want to hear the truth.

"I'll talk to Billy's and David's parents. We take bullying very seriously," Principal Harper said right away.

Great. That was the last thing I needed on top of everything else, Billy and David being blamed for bullying and my whole team hating me.

Principal Harper flipped to a business card in his Rolodex. "And I'll call the town psychic's office; we'll have someone put up an additional ward and check the school's sigils just to be sure nothing's gotten inside."

Dad's eyes nearly bulged out of his head—like the thought of a ghost in the school would make my "condition" worse. It's not that we'd never had a nasty ghost in school before; we had—but it had been years. And when we had, they'd evacuated all Untouched and brought in the federal psychics. "Mr. Lenard, I think you should take Alex home for the rest of the day." He handed Dad something small and made of glass.

A wave of panic crashed over me. The holy water bottle. I'd forgotten it on the bathroom floor.

"What's this?" Dad read the label with a gasp.

"The janitor found it in the bathroom among the broken glass. We thought it might be Alex's, maybe something to comfort him because of what happened with his mother . . ." Principal Harper shifted uncomfortably.

Dad took the bottle and stuffed it in his pocket.

"Take him home and let him rest."

"Oh, I will." Dad led me out of the office and didn't bother to look back once until we were standing outside the car.

I expected Dad to scream or blame or question. But he didn't. The anger from Principal Harper's office had vanished into a thin, tortured silence.

Dad leaned over the roof of the car, holding the nearly empty bottle of holy water between us. "Come on, champ. Whatever happened—you can tell me." Dad had that look in his eyes. The look that says he cares, but that he's totally afraid of what might come out of my mouth.

I rested my palms on the car's cool, metal roof, tracing one of the inscribed sigils with my index finger. Aunt Elena had proof. I had witnesses. Could we convince Dad that I could really see ghosts? That I'm really a psychic? I let a slow breath out through my nose. "No, Dad. I can't."

"Why not? Who else are you going to be able to talk to if not me?"

"You'll never believe me."

"Try me. And you'd better start with the truth if you want this back." Dad held up the bottle of holy water.

The truth? Dad didn't want the truth. Not really. But he wouldn't let it go. Not this time. I took a deep breath and pushed back every ounce of fear and doubt I'd had since all this craziness began. "Okay . . . you remember how I was seeing things . . . seeing ghosts?"

Dad's face went pale. "You can't see ghosts. No one in our family has ever been psychic. Including you. You're not one of those criminals who tried to destroy the world with their séances and are now fighting to put the spirits back where they belong. Their kind can never make up for what they did. You are Untouched."

I clenched my teeth and looked at Dad. "Look, I know you think I've got post-traumatic stress or something. But I don't. And I know you think psychics are nothing more than legal criminals—"

"They are. If it weren't for them, the Unleashing wouldn't have happened. People died because of them."

"The psychics who did that are dead." I could hardly believe I was defending psychics when my mom had spent her life digging up occult history to help the Untouched battle against what they'd done. "The psychics today are only trying to help. Mom would've understood. I'll bet you couldn't stand that she studied the occult, could you?" I took a huge gulp of air and tossed my hands in the air. "Psychics are not bad people. They're just people. People who see and hear ghosts. It's not like they have a choice about becoming psychic. And I know kids aren't supposed to become psychic after they turn ten, but I did. I don't know how and I don't know why. But I did see Mom in the hospital." I held up her amulet, which dangled around my neck. "That's how I got this. She gave it to me. Not the nurse."

Dad opened his mouth, but I charged on. "There's a ghost in our house. There are ghosts at school. And I can see them. The feds don't have them under control like they want everyone to believe. Sooner or later you're going to have to face it."

"I'll tell you what I have to face." Dad's cheeks reddened and his voice quivered. "I have to face losing clients and sales that we need because my son thinks he sees ghosts. We have the town's top psychics warding our homes and schools and there's no way there are spirits in both places at once. Becoming a psychic at twelve? It's ridiculous. Even ten is old. All this is in your mind because you can't get over the fact your mother is dead."

His words hit me like a sledgehammer right in the chest, making the already gaping hole there even wider.

Dad's face immediately softened, like he couldn't believe what he'd just said. I know I couldn't. "Alex . . . I'm sorry."

I shook my head, chest throbbing with the ache of losing Mom made even worse by hearing him say it. "No, you're not. You've moved on. I haven't. I won't—ever. She was my mother."

"And she was my wife," Dad snapped, some of his anger returning.

"Yeah she was . . . and I know she's—dead. But that doesn't mean I'm not telling you the truth. And it doesn't mean I'm imagining things."

Dad rubbed his hand across his forehead, fury and concern battling for first place. "Not this again, champ."

"I'm not your champ. Not anymore. Don't you get it? When Mom got killed in the car accident, everything changed. I changed. I don't play ghostball. I don't hang out with my teammates. I don't do anything normal anymore because I'm not normal. I can see ghosts. I can hear them. Not just now and then. Every day. At home. At school. And they're not in my head." I yanked down my collar and pointed at the claw marks on my neck. "A ghost did this to me. A ghost broke the mirrors. A ghost broke my windows."

"Stop. Just stop." Dad's voice came out in a hiss.

He might be angry, but I was angrier. He asked for it, and now he was getting it. "No. You wanted the truth and that's what I'm telling you."

"Oh, I hear what you're telling me. You're telling me that I'm not spending enough time with you. So you're resorting to breaking mirrors, scratching your own neck, and making up stories to get my attention." Dad thumped the roof of the car with a palm. "Well, Alex. You have my attention. All of it." Dad's fist tightened around my bottle of holy water. "I had to leave an important client meeting to come here. And now the principal thinks—I don't know what he thinks. But you've broken out two bedroom windows, now school mirrors. What's next? I will not have you hurting yourself."

"I'm not doing it." I shouted so loudly that a bird in a nearby tree flapped into the air with a screech, and two teachers out on break strained their necks to make sure no students were trying to kill each other.

Dad lowered his voice. "You're going to see Dr. Midgley on Monday morning. We're going to get to the bottom of this. I'll not have our lives swallowed up by—"

"By what? By Mom's death? You don't get to move on and pretend none of this happened. I still love her."

Dad slammed his hand into the roof of the car, leaving a fist-sized dent.

"I love her, too," Dad hissed. "Now get in the car. And you are going to see Dr. Midgley. First thing. Monday."

I opened my mouth to argue, but Dad threw his lanky self into the car and slammed the door. Great. Dad was in denial, but I knew I'd changed. I knew I was psychic. I knew that unless Elena and Frank helped me put a stop to my evil visitor, I was in deep trouble.

Chapter Thirteen

I shoved open the door to Aunt Elena's office with an annoyed kick, making the entry chimes tinkle and my hip scar scream. With my scratched arm and clawed neck, I'd almost forgotten about my gimpy leg—almost.

Hannah and Jason stood looking over an advanced warding book. I could barely believe it; Jason was here with her? He was my best friend, not Hannah's. Why was he with her? Why hadn't he waited for me after school? His betrayal stabbed me in the gut, and I tried to ignore the fact that I'd had to leave school early with Dad. Maybe Jason had tried to find me after school. Maybe they both had, but I wasn't there. I was at home pleading with Dad to let me go to Hannah's so I could catch up on any homework I'd missed. More like ghost work.

As soon as Jason and Hannah saw me they bolted straight for me. "What happened at school today?" Hannah asked, breathless.

"Everyone said that you broke mirrors and terrorized Billy and David." Jason snorted back a laugh. "I wish I'd have seen whatever you did to them. I overheard Tommy Lord say that David was crying in the school office."

"I don't give a flip about Billy and David. And they should be scared—" I glared, still angry that Jason hadn't come to my house right after school, but had decided to hang out with Hannah instead.

Hannah's mouth dropped into the shape of a large egg. "Alex, what happened to your neck?"

Aunt Elena appeared out of nowhere, which probably meant she'd been in the back storeroom and that would account for the dust in her hair. "Alex Lenard." She spun me to face her and studied the marks on my neck with a frown. "Finger marks. Scratches. They're usually not this strong," she mumbled to herself. "Did you use the holy water?"

"Yep. And salt. He couldn't get into the house last night, but he broke the windows again and my dad thinks I'm doing it. Then he attacked me at school and blew out the bathroom mirrors." I sighed. "The principal's confused, and my dad thinks I'm desperate for attention."

"I'd talk to your father if I thought it would help." Aunt Elena gave me a pitying look. "But it won't."

"Why does he hate psychics so much?" Hannah looked genuinely confused. "They're helping with the Problem. It's not like they're hurting anyone. Even if it is their fault the ghosts came through in the first place."

Elena sighed, running her fingers through the tangles in her wavy hair. "When your dad was ten, his best friend, Jeff, tested as psychic. Chris was so excited. His best friend was psychic. They stayed in touch. Jeff shared what he could about his new life and they saw each other on holidays. But then, when they were eleven, Jeff was killed by a malevolent spirit during a training exercise. Ever since then your father has hated ghosts. Hated psychics. Hated anything that has to do with the Problem. He hates what they did to Jeff and to the world."

I could barely believe it. Dad had never told me. Everything made so much more sense now. No wonder Mom never talked to him about her work.

Aunt Elena grabbed her purse. "Come on, kids. We're going to see Mr. Graves."

Hannah gasped and I looked at Jason, wondering if he knew anything about Mr. Graves. But he shrugged.

"Who?" I didn't like the sound of this.

"The cemetery caretaker. Harry Graves. We're not on the best terms since your mother's funeral, but he knows more about the comings and goings of spirits than nearly anyone else around here, including the town psychics."

Hannah bounced up and down and up and down all the way along the sidewalk to the wrought-iron cemetery gate. Large wrought-iron sigils coiled around the gate and cemetery fencing. Framing the gates were two large flickering gas lamps. They were always filled and on. No electricity was allowed in cemeteries. There were protection sigils, as well as those designed to bind spirits so they wouldn't leave the graveyard. And over the cemetery's gated entry dangled a lone God's eye of bright purple.

We stopped beneath the God's eye. Aunt Elena whispered a prayer and ward of protection. I touched Mom's Nazar Boncuğu for luck. And Hannah kept bouncing.

"Would you please stop that," I snapped, annoyed at the thudding of her heels slapping against the concrete.

"I don't like Mr. Graves. He's creepy." Hannah wrapped her jacket tightly around her.

"He's not creepy. He's old." Aunt Elena led us through the gates, toward the small caretaker's cottage.

Hannah snorted. "Older than dirt and not nearly as pretty."

"Hannah," Aunt Elena scolded. "He's eighty years old."

"Wow. That is old." Jason's eyebrows rose dramatically.

"I still say he's creepy." Hannah twirled her hair around her finger and popped the end in her mouth.

"Well, he does spend a lot of time outdoors," Aunt Elena said. "Maybe that's why he's so wrinkly. He's been taking care of the place for over fifty years."

Aunt Elena knocked at the cottage door, which was inscribed with masses of complex sigils. The door swung open and a skeletally thin man with a weathered face appeared. It was the same man who'd beckoned to me from the cemetery on my walk that day. I shivered.

"Mr. Graves." Aunt Elena went inside first with a small nod.

"Elena." His voice creaked like an old door. "Who've you brought with you?" he asked, peering over his fingerprint-smudged spectacles.

Aunt Elena pulled Hannah forward and glared at her until she shook Mr. Graves's outstretched hand. "You remember my niece, Hannah?"

"Of course." A yellowing nail scraped Hannah's hand and she recoiled, tucking herself behind me and Jason.

Jason immediately extended his hand. "Jason Anderson. Nice to meet you, sir." His lips quivered into an I-can't-believe-I'm-touching-him smile.

"And you are?" growled Mr. Graves, looking straight at me.

I swallowed the glob of slimy mucus that stuck in my throat. "Alex—Alex Lenard," I croaked. Hannah was right: Mr. Graves was totally creepy.

"Ah." Mr. Graves's nearly opaque blue eyes glistened. "Yes. I was very sorry about your mother." Spit sprayed from between his teeth, landing on my cheek and dripping onto my faded ghostball T-shirt. "The yard's been quivering with excitement about you since she died."

"The yard?" I asked before I could stop myself.

"The graveyard, boy. It tells me things. They tell me things." He glanced at the scratches on my arms and neck, then made a tutting sound with his tongue. "Don't need some town psychic or PI to tell me what's going on with the dead," he snorted, still peering at me. "Someone's not happy with you. Not happy at all."

"Right." Elena stepped forward. "Which is why we're here. We need your assistance, Mr. Graves."

"Again?" His eyes pierced hers, but Aunt Elena didn't back down, her gaze steady. Finally, Mr. Graves walked around his metal desk, sat in his beat-up office chair, and put his hands together like a steeple. "Well, then, why don't you tell me what the spirits haven't."

And Elena did. She told him about Mom and the accident. About my ability. About the house we'd investigated and what I'd seen and heard.

About the missing key. About attacks at home and school. I quietly thanked God for my aunt and let her do all the talking.

Mr. Graves leaned back in his chair, closed his eyes, and listened. When Aunt Elena finally finished he stayed that way. He was so still I could have sworn he'd died right there in his cracked leather chair.

Jason leaned close to me and whispered, "Do you think he's dead?"

I shrugged and tried not to laugh, my annoyance at Jason forgotten. "I wondered the same thing."

Aunt Elena gave me a scowl and Mr. Graves opened his eyes. "I'm not dead yet. I'm thinking."

Mr. Graves rummaged around in his desk, pulled out a tarnished flask, and took a long swig. "I think I know who you're dealing with . . . but the yard hasn't been talking. Not about that. It was a long time ago. I was still a young man then, but I remember it clear as day."

He looked from Aunt Elena to Hannah to Jason, and then he swung his chilly gaze on me. "I'll bet you dollars to cobwebs that it's Eleanor Wilkes you found in that basement wall. Neighbors said she wouldn't up and leave. Not with her new grandbaby just arrived. And she and her daughter were close. Most folks said her husband did it. Harold Wilkes. Mean old coot." Mr. Graves spat into a rusted coffee can near his feet that was filled with something black and goopy.

I shuddered. Mr. Graves wasn't just creepy. He was gross.

"We'd never go there to trick-or-treat on account of Mr. Wilkes. All the kids in the neighborhood would skip that house. He handed out hot pennies one year—straight out of the oven. Burned all our fingers. And that was that. No more trick-or-treaters for the Wilkeses. Wasn't long after that Mrs. Wilkes disappeared."

"That's awful," Hannah stammered.

"That was him, Hannah, dear. Awful. It's what he was. After Mrs. Wilkes disappeared, Old Man Wilkes didn't leave the house. Not much anyway. Never saw his daughter or his grandbaby. His daughter wouldn't even visit 'im. I think she knew he killed her mother. But no one ever found the body. And when Mr. Wilkes was laid to rest over yonder, I never did catch a glimpse of him." Mr. Graves spat another gooey glob into the can. "I supposed he became part of the Problem."

"What do you mean?" I asked.

"When folks die I usually see 'em. If they're not wanderin' around all confused and lost, sometimes they come to their funerals. See who's attending. Who's not. Then they cross over peacefully. Not many stay here. But some do. Some don't know they're dead. Others are just too afraid of what they'll find on the other side. It's them that become part of the Problem."

Was Mom wandering around the graveyard at night? Alone?

Mr. Graves turned his X-ray eyes on me. "I haven't seen your mother, son."

I was startled at the compassion in those old, glassy eyes and sense of comfort wrapped itself around me. "That's good." I wanted to cry, but pushed back tears.

"Haven't seen her, nor have the others. They'd have told me if she were lingering." Mr. Graves took a long drink from a silver flask he kept in his desk. "Too much tragedy in death. But more for those of us left living. Most spirits cross over. They go where they need to go. You'll see your mother again. Just not here."

I was relieved and crushed at the same time. I was glad Mom had crossed over. I hoped she was in the beautiful version of heaven that she believed in. But my heart broke that I'd have to go my entire life without ever seeing her again. At least now I knew she was somewhere safe. Somewhere good. Maybe that's why I'd received this "gift" as Aunt Elena called it. Maybe I was supposed to help lost souls find their way to a better place.

Aunt Elena interrupted my thoughts, reminding me of the more pressing matter of putting an end to my visits from Mr. Wilkes. "The Wilkeses' grandson, Gary Barrett, owns the house. He's the one we're investigating for."

Mr. Graves coughed and spat another glob into his tin can. "Trying to sell the old Wilkes place, is he? Old Man Wilkes'll never let it happen."

"I believe he's been trying to rent it out," said Aunt Elena quietly. "But no one will stay."

Mr. Graves leered at us. "And no wonder. A PI and a baby psychic trying to rid yourselves of that mean old spirit with salt and holy water."

Aunt Elena stiffened. "Frank Martinez is helping me. And Mr. Barrett's already got the house on OPI's waiting list and the town psychics did nothing. So he called me." She sounded indignant, but I wanted to hear what Mr. Graves had to say.

Mr. Graves looked straight at me again. "He's been attacking you, and no one else?"

"Yes, sir. That's right," I mumbled. "Except he . . . he hurt or killed the old school janitor ghost, Mr. Thomas, when he tried to protect me."

"Wilbur Thomas?" Mr. Graves's voice quivered.

I nodded.

"Good man, Wilbur Thomas. Came up here years ago from Baton Rouge. I'm not surprised he's still hangin' around that school. He loved it as much as life. His spirit may have been injured. Maybe had some of the energy drained from it. But you can't kill a ghost, son." Mr. Graves sounded confident, but his foot thumped worriedly against the edge of his desk. "He may come back—eventually." The old caretaker pulled out a chart of the cemetery and tapped his finger against one of the plot marks. "You've got to put Mrs. Wilkes to rest, boy, then we can take care of her murdering coot of a husband."

"And how are we supposed to do that?" Jason asked before I could get the words out.

"The bones, boy. You've got ta bury the bones."

Of course we did. Now all we had to do was explain to Mr. Wilkes's estranged grandson that we didn't have a simple haunting. That we had to destroy his century-old basement wall, find his murdered grandmother's bones, bury them, and get the ghosts to cross over. All without OPI or a town psychic. And we'd have to do it before Dad dragged me back to the shrink on Monday. I only hoped Mr. Barrett wouldn't mind having a renovation project to deal with in exchange for the ghosts.

Mr. Graves pointed a finger at me. "You bury her bones and you'll stand a chance of sending Old Man Wilkes on his way, too. Until Mrs. Wilkes is at peace, there's no way you'll force him to cross over."

Chapter Fourteen

We'd all gone back to Aunt Elena's office to regroup. Aunt Elena rummaged through cabinets, Hannah and Jason chattered with excitement, and I wanted to run away. How in Solomon's name was I supposed to find and bury Mrs. Wilkes's bones, convince her to cross over, and then get Mr. Wilkes to leave all without Dad knowing what we were up to? This was nuts. Totally, completely nuts. Dad would disown me if he found out.

"So what's the plan?" Hannah leaned forward, still bouncing her legs up and down. Boy, that meeting with Mr. Graves had her riled up.

"I'm going to call Frank. We'll need his help when we go back to the Wilkeses' house." Aunt Elena made a note on a slip of paper.

The thought of going back into that house made me want to move to a different state. Maybe that's what I should do.

"We'll go and speak to Mr. Barrett first thing tomorrow morning. If he wants to rent out his house or sell it, then he'll let us do what needs to be done," said Aunt Elena, her voice firm.

"And if he doesn't?" I asked. I had to. It's not like I wanted to go back into that pit of terror, but I knew I couldn't let Mr. Wilkes keep stalking me either.

"He'll do whatever it takes to get rid of what's haunting his house. If we're successful with this case, word will get around, and I'll have more business than I can handle." Aunt Elena looked determined.

Was everything about business for her? Geez.

She gave me a squeeze. "In the meantime, Alex, we need to keep you safe."

Okay . . . so maybe it wasn't just business. Maybe she really did care.

Aunt Elena walked to an antique cabinet and opened the doors. She pulled out a new bag of salt, another bottle of holy water, and some incense. "The best defense against ghosts, especially mean ones, is to neutralize your fear."

"Neutralize my fear? That's kind of hard to do when he's strangling the air out of me." It sounded harder than I meant, but come on. Old Man Wilkes was trying to kill me.

"What we need is a plan," said Aunt Elena, any trace of fear or reluctance gone. "Jason, ask your mom if Alex can spend the night at your house tonight and you tell them you'll be staying with Alex."

"Hang on." Jason shuffled back a step. "You want me to lie to my parents?"

I nearly laughed. The last time Jason had lied to his mom was when he didn't want to get in trouble for leaving inky fingerprints all over her newly painted walls. Of course, we'd both stamped our fingers on the ink pad and had "decorated" the wall, and she knew it. We'd both been scolded for ruining the wall, but the swat she'd landed on his backside was for lying.

"No, but unless you want to tell them you'll be spending the night with Hannah warding off a ghost, then you don't have many options."

"You have a point." Jason picked up the old dial phone Aunt Elena kept in her office, probably since it didn't need electricity to operate. "I'm on it."

"Good." Aunt Elena rummaged around the cabinets and pulled out several white candles. "If we're all under one roof we can take turns keeping watch—but be sure to leave out any mention of the paranormal. We don't need my brother challenging us. And right now, what Alex needs most are friends and family around who can help protect him and keep him calm. Malevolent spirits gain control by isolating the one they're attacking. By keeping their victim alone, they create more fear. And they feed on fear."

What Aunt Elena said made lots of sense. And if I didn't have to face Old Man Wilkes alone, I'd definitely be less afraid—even if I was the only one who could see the ghost.

Not surprisingly, Dad hadn't readily agreed to a sleepover at Jason's house on account of my "drama" at school. But in the end, Dad agreed that hanging out with my best friend might do me some good. That it might bring some normalcy back to my life. So, after a quick trip home to repack my bag and recheck the sigils on my ghostball trap, I headed back to Hannah's.

Hannah opened the front door and her face lit up. Nerves crawled up and down my spine and I set my backpack next to the front door. Maybe spending the night here wasn't such a good idea . . .

"Hey." Jason came out of the kitchen with a mouthful of something. I almost laughed. Leave it to Jason to eat no matter what the circumstances. "There's some mac 'n' cheese and sweet plantains in the kitchen if you want some. Mom sent me over with enough food for an army." Food sprayed out of his mouth while he talked.

Hannah wrinkled her nose. "Close your mouth and chew, please."

Jason popped another plantain into his mouth and chewed noisily.

"My mom's already in her room. Friday's her night to lock herself in, have wine, and watch movies until she passes out. So we won't be hearing from her at all." Hannah's voice said she was cool with it, but the droop in her shoulders gave away how she really felt. It sucked that her dad had left, and that on Fridays her mom left, too. But her face brightened when Aunt Elena walked in the room. I guess it made sense that Hannah put so much energy into Aunt Elena and the PI stuff. It was always there for her.

"And thank goodness for your mother's Friday night television-wine ritual. We don't need her snooping around in here." Aunt Elena struck a match, lit her lantern candle, and led us into the front room where a dozen or so white pillar candles flickered in the near darkness.

"Why are all the lights out in here?" There's no way I was going to take part in some sort of séance.

Aunt Elena set down the lantern and handed me a small plastic pouch with what looked like rock salt and herbs. "I don't want to give Mr. Wilkes any extra help getting inside. Now, you, go and take a bath."

"Excuse me?" A bath was the last thing on my list to do at Hannah's house.

Jason and Hannah busted out laughing. I scowled at them both. Especially Jason. "Traitor," I hissed at him. He'd never chattered on so much with anyone but me—especially not a girl . . . who happened to be my weirdo PI cousin. I shook my head, trying to wrap my mind around it.

Aunt Elena gave me a gentle prod toward the bathroom. "Go take a bath with the sea salt, sage, and rosemary. It will help protect you from Mr. Wilkes. The bath's already drawn."

Collecting the lantern and my backpack, I headed toward the bathroom and wondered what they'd be talking about while I was gone.

"And put this on when you're done." Aunt Elena handed me a small silver pendant. A Seal of Solomon. The same one tattooed at the base of Frank's throat. "It's a Third Pentacle of Saturn. It will help protect you against evil spirits."

I put the pendant around my neck where it clanked against Mom's amulet. I hoped between the two, I'd be safe. I closed the bathroom door to the chatter of Hannah and Jason and inhaled steam that wafted up from the tub. I couldn't remember feeling this relaxed since—well, to be honest, since before Mom died. I set the lantern on the vanity and my backpack on the back of the toilet, then let my clothes drop in a heap on the bathroom floor. I dumped the salt mixture into the pre-drawn bath, then slipped in. The warm water and fragrance of the sage and rosemary wrapped around me, soothing the sore muscles of my injured leg. Melting away the worry and anticipation and fear from my mind.

Maybe I really would sleep well tonight. With Aunt Elena and Jason and Hannah keeping watch, I had to, right?

I inhaled the steam. The flickering candlelight made my eyes flutter. My shoulders relaxed and I slid deeper into the bath.

Eeeeee—Eeeeee—Eeeeee . . .

The steam swirled so thickly I could hardly see across the white-tiled bathroom.

Eeeee—Eeeeee—Eeeee . . .

The sound of a wet finger on glass. I stared, hard, but could barely make out the mirror.

Eeeee—Eeeee—Eeeee . . .

I swallowed the ball of fear clogging my throat, rose from the water, wrapped a fluffy white towel around my waist, and clung to the pendant Elena had given me. I trudged forward as a final letter appeared in the steamy mirror.

I CAN SEE YOU

My breath caught. There in the mirror, where I could see my reflection through the steam in the letters, emerged a face. Not my face. But the face of an old man with a scraggly beard, his mouth contorted with rage.

A deep exhale from behind raised goose bumps along my shoulder and a claw-like hand ripped the flesh on my back.

I screamed in pain, threw open the bathroom door, and dashed into the hall.

Heart thudding, I ran to the front room where Aunt Elena stood lighting the last of the candles.

"Alex, where are your clothes—" Hannah's cheeks turned pink, but I couldn't care less. I'd left my jeans in the bathroom with whoever or whatever was likely still in there and I wasn't going to go back for them.

Jason stared at me. And he wasn't laughing. "Your back is bleeding."

I raised a shaking hand and pointed. "Jeans are still in there . . ." A deep, rumbling moan echoed through the house. "With him."

Aunt Elena examined the scratches on my back, took a long, deep breath, held a smoldering bundle of sage before her, and marched straight toward Mr. Wilkes.

Chapter Fifteen

Hannah handed me and Jason bottles of holy water. "We're going in to get your clothes."

Really? We were going to do battle with a ghost over my clothes? No way. "Can't I just borrow something?"

"Oh, sure, I'll lend you an old T-shirt," Hannah scoffed. "It's got hearts and flowers on it. And it's pink."

Jason snorted back a laugh and I scowled. I'd gotten enough grief the time I'd had to borrow Jason's mom's pink princess shirt when we were kids. Nope. I'd run around shirtless before borrowing one of Hannah's or going back in that bathroom.

Hannah's eyes sparkled with laughter.

"You don't even have a pink T-shirt, do you?" I glared.

"Of course not . . . but seriously, Alex . . ." She squared her shoulders and lifted her chin high. "You can't let spirits bully you. They'll feed off your fear. You have to stand up to them."

"Strong words for someone who's never been clawed at by a ghost."

Aunt Elena stopped at the threshold to the hallway and turned back to us. "Alex. Hannah. Stop bickering. It will only give him more power. And Hannah's right. Fear will only make him stronger. Now I need your help. All of you." She nodded her head in the direction of the bathroom.

"Hang on a sec." Jason went over to his bag by the front door. "Alex, where's your backpack?"

"I left it in the bathroom, why?"

Jason's shoulders slumped. "I was going to get your ghostball trap. This is the perfect chance to try it, then maybe we won't have to simply scare away old Mr. Wilkes. Maybe we can catch him."

If we'd used the correct sigils, then it might work. And if it did? "What will we do with him if we catch him?" I wasn't ready to try to cross over some malevolent spirit.

"I'm not sure about testing out some homemade ghost trap. You boys need to let Frank look at it when he arrives. But this can't wait." Aunt Elena gestured to the bathroom. "We need to do this, now. I won't have a malevolent spirit in my house." With a look of determination that gave me a hint of comfort, I clutched my bottle of holy water tight.

"Hannah, bring the Bible. Alex and Jason, make sure your holy water is ready. We must say a prayer of cleansing. It won't likely drive him away from Alex, but hopefully it will drive him from the house. Now follow me." Elena stepped forward, smoldering sage in the lead, and began to pray. "Father in Heaven, please destroy every negative entity's connection to this house and to this boy, Alex."

The walls trembled, and pictures along the hallway began knocking together.

"Oh, mouse poop," Jason mumbled under his breath. I was too scared to laugh. Ever since we were kids, Jason had used that as his swearword on account of the time his mother had caught him using a Jamaican swearword and washed his mouth out with soap. She wouldn't complain about him saying mouse poop.

"Stop him from returning by putting a barrier of your divine power between him and all who dwell in this home," Aunt Elena kept praying, eyes focused on the bathroom door.

Aunt Elena stepped into the bathroom, Hannah, Jason, and me crowding in behind her. The mirror shook. The glass in the small bathroom window shook. Even the water in the toilet shook.

"Render any negative energy or entities around this boy or on this land powerless," Aunt Elena continued and lifted the sage over the smeared writing on the mirror and into each corner of the room.

A powerful screech, worse than an angry cat's yowl, ripped through the air.

"Hannah, the Lord's Prayer. Alex, Jason. The holy water. Now."

Hannah flipped open the Bible and began reciting without glancing at its pages. "Our Father, who Art in Heaven . . ."

I uncapped the holy water and sprinkled it behind Aunt Elena and into every corner of the room. Jason flung his at the mirror. The moan escalated into a growling wail and the bathroom mirror shattered, spilling into the sink.

Jason screamed. I fought the urge to bolt.

"In the name of Jesus Christ, I bind every negative spirit that dwells within these walls or on this land and command them to flee immediately. I take back this house in Your name, and no evil or negative spirit can enter this space forevermore."

As suddenly as the shaking started, it stopped. The wailing stopped, and the air cleared.

Aunt Elena gestured for me to get my clothes and backpack, which sat untouched on the floor. "Take them, Alex."

Jason at my back, I recapped the holy water, grabbed my clothes and bag, and sprinted into the hall. We may have gotten Old Man Wilkes out of the bathroom, but there was no way I was going to stay in there for a second longer than I had to. I'd pee in the bushes tonight instead of going back in there.

The others followed me into the living room and set down their lanterns and supplies.

A knock at the door made us all jump.

"It's Frank." Aunt Elena sounded almost as if she hadn't been so sure until he poked his head in the front door.

Frank took one look at me in my towel-backpack ensemble and said, "What happened?"

Everyone stared at me. I squirmed.

"Alex, get dressed. If Hannah's mother comes out she'll wonder what in Solomon's name is happening in this house." She turned to the rest of the group. "Frank, Hannah, Jason, you come with me into the kitchen. We'll get something to eat while Alex's dressing, and then we're going to come up with a plan."

Aunt Elena slid the kitchen door closed and I quickly pulled on my boxers, jeans, and T-shirt, then flopped down onto the sofa and wondered if I would sleep tonight.

"How you holding up?" Frank startled me. I hadn't even heard him come out of the kitchen.

"Okay," I said. I was still alive after being attacked by an evil ghost.

Frank sighed and sat beside me. "Alex, I know this is hard and you'll need some testing, but I think you're a Class A Psychic."

What? Me? A Class A Psychic? "How is that possible?" My voice cracked.

Elbows on his knees, Frank leaned forward, his brows furrowed in thought, his gargoyle tattoo's eyes bulging out at me. "Elena has told me what you've seen and heard. She's excited about what you can do."

"Yeah. I'm sure she is. If I really am as psychic as she thinks I am, then I'll be great for business," I said with a scowl.

Frank sighed. "She won't push you. She's your aunt. And believe it or not she really does want what's best for you." Frank looked at me closely. "You're good with sigils. And I pick up certain energy from you that makes me think that's the case."

"Will you test me?" I blurted. I didn't want to be tested, but if anyone had to do it, I'd rather it be Frank right here in my hometown. The last thing I wanted was to be shipped off to some institute.

He set his jaw. "I'm not in the training business anymore. I'm retired."

"But—"

"No buts," Frank said matter-of-factly.

I frowned. If I got out of this situation without anyone finding out about my new abilities, I'd be lucky.

"Elena and Jason showed me the ghostball trap you boys created. Ingenious. You chose some good sigils for drawing a spirit to the trap and for protecting yourself, but you will need to use an activation ward to make it work." Frank pulled something out of his jacket pocket.

"Activation ward?"

He held a slim, tattered book in his hand entitled Ghost Hunting: A Psychic's Manual. "I've used this for years. It's still the best resource on ghost hunting I've found."

He flipped the book open to a page covered in handwritten scrawl. "This is a ward of drawing and protection dating back to the time of King Solomon."

I took the book and read:

By the light
On this day/night
I call to Thee
To give me Your might.
By the power of three
I call to Thee
Into the (name of your trap)
Lord protect all
That surround me
So may it be
So may it be.

"And this will help me draw the spirit into the ball?" I offered the book back to Frank.

He pushed it back into my hands. "You keep it. That simple ward is one of the best I've found to draw a spirit and garner protection. Memorize it. It may come in handy if you have to use your ghostball trap. After this one, flip to page twenty-three and memorize the ward-prayer for helping reluctant spirits cross over."

I studied the ward.

"Well, say it to me," Frank commanded.

"Um, okay." I cleared my throat and read aloud. "By the light, on this . . ."

"If it's day, you say day; if it's night, you say night." Frank scowled like I was an idiot.

"On this night," I continued, "I call to Thee to give me Your might. By the power of three, I command Thee into this ghostball?"

Frank nodded. "You'd hold your trap toward the spirit."

"Lord protect all that surround me. So may it be. So may it be."

"Good. Now make sure you have that one and the prayer of crossing over memorized before we go into the Wilkes house tomorrow. I have a feeling you'll need them."

So the plan was, after a good night's sleep, we'd talk to Mr. Barrett to get approval to tear open his basement wall, and then regroup at Aunt Elena's office with Frank. Then we'd do the clearing.

"I still don't understand why it has to be me asking for permission," I groaned. I didn't want to ask the grandson of a murderer if I could clear his house. Heck, I didn't even know how to clear a house.

"Because you're the psychic and you're the one being attacked." Hannah said it as though it were the most obvious thing in the world. "And Frank says you need the practice."

"We'll be with you." Jason gave me one his reassuring, I've-got-your-back smiles.

"And the more involved you are with clearing the house, the more power we'll have to help move Mr. Wilkes along." Aunt Elena sounded confident. "And we can't just break down the basement wall without permission."

Jason and I spread out our sleeping bags on the sofas in the front room and Hannah tossed each of us a pillow.

"I sleep in there." My aunt pointed to an open doorway, through which I saw antique-looking maroon wallpaper with sigils. I shivered. "My door will be open. If you need me."

"What about me?" Hannah pushed her lips into a pout, a pillow and blanket in her arms.

"I'm sure you'll be much more comfortable in your bedroom." There was no way Aunt Elena was going to let Hannah sack out with a couple of boys. And I was glad.

"But—"

"Just leave your door open. We'll call if we need you." Aunt Elena's tone left no room for argument. "Now let's all go to sleep. We have a big day ahead of us tomorrow."

Frank had already passed out in a front-room chair. Head tilted back, he was snoring softly.

Clothes still on, Jason snuggled into his sleeping bag, and I climbed into mine, drawing it up to my chin. It reminded me of all our summer camping trips with his dad—except, of course, we were inside a house, not in the woods, and we had to use extra wards to protect us from a murderous ghost.

"Night, J," I said, suddenly very glad he was there. Very glad I hadn't pushed away the best friend I'd ever had. "Thanks for being here for me . . . despite all the craziness."

The only response was the faint whirring of Jason's breath. Asleep. I grinned. Jason could sleep anywhere.

I rolled on my side so I had a view of my aunt's room. I touched the pendant she'd given me and my finger stroked the cool, smooth glass of

Mom's amulet. A shiver shot through me. Why had Mom given me her amulet? Had she somehow known I'd become psychic in the accident? Maybe she knew I'd need the extra protection. She may have been an occult historian, but she believed in her wards and sigils and charms. Always. She knew the tricks spirits could get up to. She'd studied it anyway. My stomach did a flip-flop. I didn't want to be a psychic. I wanted everything to go back to the way it was. Mom. Dad. Me. Home. I clenched my teeth and let the reality of my new life settle over me. Sort of like a nettle that gets stuck on the inside of your sock. It totally sucks.

Well, at least I was surrounded by friends and holy water and salt. Hopefully, the night would be peaceful. I was so tired that it wasn't long before my eyes drooped closed and I had the first good night of sleep I'd had in weeks.

Chapter Sixteen

Morning came quickly, and before I knew it, I was in the Lower Garden District knocking on the front door of the old Wilkes place, peeling white paint lodging itself under my fingernails.

Frank had gone back to his office to make some final preparations, but Aunt Elena stood to my right and Hannah to my left. And, as usual, Jason had my back. Somehow I'd become the leader of this paranormal expedition and I didn't like it. Maybe I was psychic, but it's not like I had a clue what I was doing. Aunt Elena had taken on the case. Aunt Elena was paid to clear the house. Aunt Elena was the paranormal expert. Not me.

The sound of tires on gravel made us all turn.

A Cadillac squealed to a stop and Mr. Barrett, a tubby man with a worried face and thinning gray hair, heaved himself out of the car.

He slammed his car door and teetered up the steps and onto the porch, hand extended to Aunt Elena. "Sorry I'm late. I didn't really want to be alone in there anyway, you know?" He chuckled.

Did this idiot know what we were up against?

Aunt Elena shook Mr. Barrett's hand.

"You brought your kids today. So the place must be safe now, right?" Sweat glistened on Mr. Barrett's balding head despite the early autumn breeze.

"Not quite. We've identified the source of the haunting—and it is a haunting—but we need to . . ." Elena hesitated. "Would you like to go inside so we can discuss this?"

"No. No, I'm fine right here. As you know, the town psychics couldn't handle it. They wanted to bring in another group from out of town, but that group wanted to charge a fortune. Blasted psychics. And the feds." Mr. Barrett tossed up his hands. "OPI has me on a waiting list. So, no. The town psychics warned me to keep my distance. If that thing is still in there, I'm not going in."

Whoa. If the town psychics couldn't handle it, why in Solomon's name had Elena taken the case? She wasn't even a registered psychic. My confidence drained out of me like I was a spaghetti sieve. Was she trying to get us killed all for the sake of building her business?

Mr. Barrett frowned up at the house then back at Aunt Elena. "Maybe I should have waited for the OPI to send someone." Sweat trickled off his forehead and into his eye.

Aunt Elena exhaled through her nose, obviously annoyed. "I realize the town psychics were unable to dislodge the spirit of Mr. Wilkes. However, I have other skills and a partner who previously worked for OPI. We can handle it." She pulled me forward by the elbow. "Mr. Barrett, this is Alex Lenard. And he's taking the lead on this case."

My insides felt like Mr. Barrett's face looked—sick. Aunt Elena was definitely trying to get us killed.

"He—he's what? He's just a kid," Mr. Barrett stammered. "Where's your partner?"

"My partner will be present for the clearing. Alex may be a kid, but he's also the strongest psychic I've ever met. And we'll need him to help your grandmother cross over and put your grandfather to rest."

"My—my grandfather?" A stutter I hadn't noticed before colored Mr. Barrett's words and he ran his stubby fingers through his thinning hair. "It—it can't be . . ."

"It is . . . and to make sure he's gone, we need your permission to open up the basement wall."

"To do what?" A vein throbbed so hard in Mr. Barrett's neck that I thought he might have a heart attack. That's just what we needed, another Wilkes family ghost on our hands.

"Mr. Barrett," my voice sounded more confident than I felt. "An angry spirit, who we believe is your grandfather, has taken an interest in attacking me."

"And why in Solomon's name would he do that?" Mr. Barrett gulped.

Before I could respond, another Cadillac pulled up the gravel drive, tossing dust into the air, and a thin, elderly woman stepped out.

"Momma?" Mr. Barrett's eyebrows rose and the old woman in wobbly high heels crunched through the gravel toward us. "I told you I'd handle this."

"It's my house, Gary." She tromped up onto the porch. "I have a right to know what's going on. Even if I don't live here."

Mr. Barrett took a step back, giving her space.

Hands on her hips, Mrs. Barrett, the Wilkeses' very own daughter, looked Elena straight in the eyes. "Tell me everything."

Aunt Elena repeated what she'd already told Mr. Barrett, then took a deep breath and I continued for her. "And we think he's attacking me because I heard the terrified spirit of a woman in the basement. She was trapped and afraid," I told the Wilkeses' sweaty lump of a grandson, then turned to his sharp-eyed mother. "I think your father killed your mother and buried her body in the basement wall so no one would find her."

Mr. Barrett's face went pale. He opened his mouth. Closed it.

Mrs. Barrett's lips drew into a grim line. "All these years . . . we thought he killed her." She swallowed. "I knew he did it. But we never had proof." Tears formed in her bright eyes. "I knew Mama wouldn't up and leave. Not with Gary just being born."

Her gaze floated to the basement window. "And if you do find her—find Mama—then what?"

Aunt Elena put a reassuring hand on Mrs. Barrett's shoulder and squeezed. "Then Mr. Graves will bury her and we'll help her cross over. She'll find peace."

"And my father?" Mrs. Barrett's lips hardened.

Aunt Elena hesitated, then spoke slowly. "That will be more difficult . . . but between the four of us and my partner, I'm sure we can put him to rest."

Mr. Barrett wiped his moist forehead with a crumpled handkerchief and shoved it back in his pocket. "I don't know, Momma . . . They could make a big mess digging out the basement wall. It could cost—"

Mrs. Barrett raised her hand. "If it will make this house livable again. If it will bring peace to my mama—" She thought about it and nodded. "I will pay it. That would make me happy. To know my mama's at peace. Your grandma deserves that. And more." She nodded at me, then Aunt Elena. "If it's possible, do it."

"But—" Gary Barrett gaped.

"No buts." She took her son firmly by the arm and they walked down the porch steps, stopping just short of their cars.

Mr. Barrett wiped a trail of dusty sweat from his forehead and called back to us. "Just try not to cause too much damage, okay?"

We returned to her office by eleven o'clock. Aunt Elena confirmed the meeting place and time with Frank, and Jason and I headed home to grab lunch with Dad.

"We're going to hang out with Hannah and watch movies . . . I'm supposed to go back over there around two o'clock." I shoved half of a grilled cheese sandwich in my mouth. With all of the excitement, I hadn't had dinner last night or breakfast this morning, and I was starving.

Jason obviously was, too; he snarfed down his second sandwich before I'd finished my first.

Dad watched us suspiciously. "Slow down. Both of you." He pushed his own sandwich toward me. "Have mine. I'll make another."

"Great." I took another bite and tried to chew more slowly.

"Can I have another one, too?" Jason mumbled over a half-chewed mouthful.

Dad dropped a dab of butter on the hot pan with a hiss and prepared the bread and cheese. "I think you should tell Hannah thank you, but that you'll catch a movie with her some other time."

"What? No." I swallowed a mouthful. "I mean why?"

"After all the excitement at school yesterday, I rescheduled my Saturday showings so we can spend some time together. What do you say, cham—" He stopped himself midword.

Jason squirmed and I cringed. "Ah, oh. Well, you didn't have to do that, you know?"

"I know, but I need to spend more time with you."

My eyes darted around the room, searching for a good excuse to get out of the unplanned father-son time. Mrs. Wilson appeared at the top of the ceiling and gave me a little wave. Where in Solomon's name had she been? I'd talk to her later. Now was not the time. "Can't we do it Sunday?"

Dad stopped cooking, spatula held in midair. "Why do you need to go and watch movies with Hannah so badly? Jason can stay and hang out with us if he wants."

"I'm finally getting to know my family—your family. It's what you wanted, right? I'm not isolating myself." I looked sidelong at Jason. "No offense, J."

Jason shrugged and shoveled another bite of sandwich into his mouth.

Dad flipped the grilled cheese from the pan to a plate and faced me, spatula in hand. "Yes, I'm glad you've become friends with your cousin. And I'm glad your grades are holding up. But that doesn't mean you get to do whatever you want, whenever you want. And after yesterday, I'm going to spend some time with you. So, call her up and tell her thank you, but no. Or I will."

Dad set his plate on the table and I stood up.

"Whatever—"

"Excuse me?"

Jason stopped chewing, eyes nearly popping out of his head.

"Mom would've let me go."

"Well I'm not your mother. And if you continue to argue, you can go to your room."

"Fine. I will." I shoved the chair into the table and stalked up the stairs. Jason could deal with Dad. If I had to pretend to be locked in my room while I snuck off to finish this Wilkes business, then so be it.

I slammed my bedroom door closed, locked it, and plopped down onto my bed. I wish I didn't have to go to the Wilkeses'. I wish I didn't have to deal with a ghost. I wish I wasn't psychic. Life as an Untouched had been so much simpler.

Just then Mrs. Wilson floated through my bedroom wall. "Where have you been, child? I've been worried about you."

"You could've fooled me," I snapped, and instantly regretted it. Ghost or not, she'd been the closest thing to a mother I'd had since Mom died. Still, she'd abandoned me when Mr. Wilkes had attacked. "You're the one who's been missing."

Mrs. Wilson sat with a huff on my bed, making a large indentation, and put her head in her translucent hands. "Oh, Alex . . . I'm so sorry. But I didn't leave you. I was hiding. That . . . that man is awful. Truly terrible."

I swallowed back the wave of guilt that crashed over me about Mr. Thomas. "I know. I think he killed, er, hurt the school janitor or something."

"He killed a man?" Her nostrils flared in alarm and her cheeks flushed pink.

"Well, sort of—he's a ghost. At school. Mr. Thomas." I was still confused about what could have happened to his spirit. There was still so much I didn't know about the paranormal. True, all Untouched lived with ghosts, but it was the psychics who really knew about them. Even paranormal investigators had limited knowledge. And Frank thought I was a Class A Psychic. Great. Why was I so lucky to be part of the elite 1 percent? Ugh. "Can ghosts kill each other?"

Mrs. Wilson's momentary relief was replaced by brows furrowed so deeply that beans could have been planted in them. "I don't know, Alex." She stood up and paced around my bedroom. "We're already dead. But strong spirits—malevolent ghosts—they're out to do harm. They can certainly hurt us. Perhaps send us to another plane of existence. But I don't think we can be any more dead than we already are."

"Mr. Thomas saved me . . ." I cleared what felt like cobwebs from my throat. "He saved me. And I was afraid of him because of the bullet holes."

Mrs. Wilson chuckled. "Afraid of Wilbur Thomas?" She patted my arm, sending goose bumps coursing over my skin. "He's one of the kindest men I ever knew." She made a clicking, tutting sound with her tongue. "Some naughty kids put bullets in the radiator, way back. When he went into work and lit the radiator the next morning, the bullets went off. Shot and killed poor Wilbur Thomas. He loved that school. Loved the kids there, too." She looked thoughtfully out the window. "I didn't know he stayed behind. Not that I'm surprised. His job and that school were his life. Not a good way to go by the hands of Mr. Wilkes. You must do something, Alex. Avenge him."

If only I'd been kinder to Mr. Thomas. He'd tried to protect me. He'd chased away Billy and David. He'd saved me from Mr. Wilkes. I didn't want to be psychic and I didn't want to deal with Mr. Wilkes, but I didn't appear to have a choice. I wasn't the ghostball champ anymore. I could see and hear ghosts. And now I had to deal with them. So, I let out a deep exhale and then told Mrs. Wilson exactly what we planned to do.

"You're going to break open the basement wall, remove Mrs. Wilkes's bones, bury them at the cemetery, and hope that Mr. Wilkes crosses over?" Mrs. Wilson paled, if it were possible for a translucent ghost to be more pale. "Have you all lost your marbles? Old Man Wilkes will be furious."

"He's already furious." A sinking feeling hit my stomach; our plan really wasn't much of a plan. "And we'll have salt and holy water and incense." And maybe my ghostball trap will come in handy if Jason and I have got the sigils right.

Wide eyed, Mrs. Wilson nibbled her pudgy, ghostly fingers. "I don't know, Alex. Maybe you should just—"

"Should just what? The OPI has the house on a waiting list. The town psychics are too afraid to go back. So what should I do? Run away and let him keep attacking me?" I stood up, barely keeping my voice below a yell. "Should I tell my dad about Old Man Wilkes? And that we're fixing to break open the tomb of his dead wife to send them both on their way?" I clenched my fists in tight knots. "Mr. Wilkes has caused enough harm. And we're not going to let him keep terrorizing people. I'm not going to let him do it."

Tears glistened in Mrs. Wilson's eyes, and I felt guilty all over again. I reached out and tried to pat her pillowy shoulders, but all I got were some slimy chills. "I know you're worried. I'm worried, too. But unless we do something he won't stop."

"Can't you just—leave?"

"My dad won't leave this place. Besides, who's to say Mr. Wilkes wouldn't follow me?" I picked up the bag of salt I'd hidden under the bed, and tilted my chin toward the ceiling. "I want you to go up to the attic until this is over. I'll salt it behind you so Mr. Wilkes can't get in. You'll be safe."

"How will I get out if something happens to you?"

"I'll be back," I said, pretending her words didn't scare me. "And if not, salt lines don't last forever. They never do."

Trembling, she followed me to the door.

I cracked it open and peeked out. Jason sat on the hallway floor, a frown on his face. "Who were you talking to?"

I looked up and down the hallway. No sign of Dad. Good. I opened the door and stepped out. "That'd be Mrs. Wilson. The ghost I told you about. She lives here."

Jason shot up onto his feet.

"She won't hurt you," I said, then looked toward the stairs. "Where's my dad?"

Jason searched the air around me, obviously not catching on to the large figure of Mrs. Wilson hovering a few feet in front of him. "Downstairs, and he isn't happy."

"Oh, well." I crept into the hall, glad he was downstairs. "I have to do something, then I'll meet you at Hannah's." Mrs. Wilson floated behind me.

"What about your dad?"

"I don't really care, but he can't interfere with our plans." I sighed, resigned that lying was the only way to deal with my dad if he wouldn't listen to the truth. "Tell him I wouldn't come out of my room. Then leave. I'll meet you at Hannah's in fifteen minutes."

Jason nodded. I knew he wouldn't want to lie to Dad, but there was no other option. He took a deep breath and headed back downstairs.

"See you soon." I turned the opposite direction and led Mrs. Wilson up to the attic where I spread salt around its periphery.

Mrs. Wilson sat on an old box of photographs and twisted her hands in her lap. "I know you have to get rid of him, Alex. Just be careful."

"I will." I nodded and dumped the last of the bag at the top of the attic stairs. I checked the sigils on the windows and made sure there was no break in my salt line. With everything in order, I turned and tried to sound as reassuring as possible. "And try not to worry, Mrs. Wilson. It'll all be over soon." One way or the other it would be over. I only hoped we'd all make it through alive.

Susan McCauley

Chapter Seventeen

I closed my bedroom door, locked it, and hefted my newly loaded backpack over both shoulders. Hopefully Dad wouldn't check my room for a while. If he believed Jason and found the door locked, he'd probably think I was still mad about him not letting me go to Hannah's.

Tossing my leg out the open window, I dropped to the roof, leapt onto an adjacent tree limb, and plopped into the yard. "Uff." I hit the ground with a thud and the scar on my hip screamed. I crouched for a minute in the shadows of the massive oaks, waiting for my leg to stop throbbing, grateful my room faced the backyard. Away from Dad's office. Away from his view.

"Pssst." A hiss from the shadowy tree line launched my heart into overdrive.

Then I saw him. Jason. He sat at an awkward angle among the shrubs outside of Hannah's house trying to look inconspicuous.

"What are you doing over there?" I limped toward him fast, silently praying Dad wasn't looking out a window.

"Waiting for you, of course." Jason stood up, wiping his dirt-stained hands on his pants. "Didn't want to go in without you."

I was glad he'd waited. I needed a friend to deal with the monster. "Did you tell my dad I wouldn't come out?"

Jason nodded. "He didn't seem surprised. He told me to give you time. Said you were still dealing with your mom's death."

It was true, even if I didn't want to hear it. "I always will be dealing with it." I touched Mom's blue amulet and hoped somehow she'd see me through what we were fixing to attempt.

"Come on. Let's get this over with." I lurched up and headed toward Hannah's front door, pausing to side-hug my best friend. "Thanks, man. I know you hate lying. But sometimes . . ."

"Yeah," he said quietly, taking the final steps to the door with me. "Sometimes . . ."

In less than an hour we had unloaded our gear in the front room of the Wilkeses' house. Aunt Elena was setting up a monitor and EMF reader when Frank walked in with two sledgehammers and a crowbar.

Maybe busting out a basement wall would be fun. Jason's face split into a grin. Looks like he thought so, too.

Hannah took out her EVP detector, flipped a switch, and started scanning the walls. "Nothing so far."

What a nerd. She should be the psychic, not me. She'd love it.

"Elena." Frank nodded to the glowing screens and gadgets in his hands. "You stay here and monitor our readings."

Elena's face hardened, but she didn't complain.

"Hannah, you can stay with your aunt or bring your EMF detector to the basement with us."

Hannah nearly bounced off the floor with delight. "I'll come."

Frank looked at her hard and she stopped bouncing. "This is serious business. Stay calm and watch the readings."

"Yes, sir."

I hoped I'd be as calm as Frank in situations like this one day. With training maybe I would be. Maybe.

Frank handed me one of the sledgehammers and gave Jason the crowbar. "You boys ready to go and break down this wall?"

I'd always imagined federal psychics to be totally brainy. I never imagined them covered in tattoos toting crowbars and hammers. The coolness factor of being a psychic just went way up. This was going to be fun.

Frank laughed as if he could read my mind. "There's a lot more to psychic fieldwork than seeing spirits. You've got a lot to learn. But for now, follow my lead and remember that prayer-ward I showed you."

I nodded and repeated it to myself before following Frank into the dark.

Silence seemed to fill every facet of the basement. No sound. No light. No movement. No chill to let me know if Mrs. Wilkes was even here. It was like I'd imagined the whole thing that night we'd been here to investigate—except that they had evidence. Her voice. My screams.

Jason flipped on his headlamp. If I weren't so scared, I would have laughed. Jason looked like some sort of freaked-out spelunker.

"Where did you feel drawn to the wall, Alex?" Frank asked, his hands outstretched, exploring the energy of the room. As a Class A Psychic, Frank could feel energies and hear and see them, just like me.

I didn't respond at first. I wanted to know if Frank felt anything.

"I feel like something traumatic happened here." He tapped the spot on the wall where I'd heard Mrs. Wilkes's fearful cries.

"That's it," I gulped. "That's the spot." A sudden chill coursed over my arms and along my spine.

Jason shivered and his breath came out in large, white puffs. "Do you feel that?" His light swung wildly around the room with his head. "It's so cold."

Frank's face grew grim and he flipped on his own headlamp. "Right. We'd best get started before we have too much activity." He hefted the sledgehammer and smashed it into the bricks. I did the same.

Bricks crumbled beneath our pounding hammers. That's when the screaming started.

"Stop. What are you doing? He'll kill you. He'll kill you all." Mrs. Wilkes's voice hitched, frantic. Her face appeared through the hole we'd broken into the wall. She was pale, translucent, but I clearly saw the bloody gash in the side of her head. The gash that had likely ended her life. I swallowed back bile, wondering how he'd done it.

Smash.

Smash.

Smash.

Our hammers and Jason's pry bar pulled away the bricks. Despite the effort, I was getting colder. Shivering.

Beep. Beep. Beep. Hannah's EVP reader pulsed loudly with every smash of our hammers. "My readings are getting stronger," she said, her voice thin and full of fear.

I knew he was coming before I heard his roar.

Frank's eyes flickered to the sound of the angry spirit, but he didn't even flinch. He simply directed his headlamp inside the hole we'd made in the wall. "Alex, quickly now. Collect her bones."

Right. I dropped my hammer and adjusted the light on my head. Why did I have to grab the bones? I didn't ask. There wasn't time.

Out of the corner of my eye I saw Jason rummaging in my backpack. He pulled out our ghostball trap and handed it to Frank. "Go for it, X. We've got this if we need it." He tossed me my now-empty backpack.

Frank and Jason faced the roaring spirit of Mr. Wilkes and I went for the bones.

I slithered inside the space we'd created in the wall and landed next to Mrs. Wilkes's long-dead corpse. There wasn't much there except for cobweb-covered bones that poked out of a faded floral dress. No skin. Not much hair. I wish I'd brought gloves.

That's when I felt her looking at me. "What are you doing, child?" she asked, her voice tight with fear. Mrs. Wilkes's spirit looked from me to her corpse.

"Hurry, Alex. He's stronger than I expected," Frank called to me. "Get that ball ready for me, Jason."

I tried not to listen to them, but focused on collecting the brittle bones. "You shouldn't be here, Mrs. Wilkes." My fingers closed around her skeletal arm, and it snapped off with the crunch of dried firewood. Gross. I pushed away my disgust and shoved her arm in the bag.

"What are you doing with those?" Her wide eyes stared at the lifeless skeleton.

"You shouldn't be here. You shouldn't be afraid of him anymore. You need to go into the light, Mrs. Wilkes. That's why we're here. We're going to bury you so you can go where you belong."

A faint look of hope crossed her face, but died when we heard a horrific roar.

Jason screamed and I grabbed at her body, shoving her other arm and legs and pelvis and spine into my backpack. There was no time to be grossed out. My friends were out there dealing with a malevolent spirit. The same malevolent spirt that had nearly got me killed.

Last, I popped her skull into the bag. "Come with me, Mrs. Wilkes. It's time to go where you belong."

Mrs. Wilkes gave a fretful nod, then, as a wispy mist, settled herself within the bag of bones. Okay, that was creepy. I tried not to shudder and climbed out of the wall. That's when my Third Pentacle of Jupiter tattoo began to itch. Not a good sign.

I'd expected Mr. Wilkes to be safely contained inside our ghostball, but what I found nearly made my blood freeze. Jason lay on the floor, a thin trail of blood dripping from his nose. Hannah and Frank stood frozen solid, locked in place, looks of terror etched on their faces like the life-size wax figures I'd seen at the Witch Dungeon Museum on our trip to Salem last year. Our ghostball trap lay unused at Frank's feet, its sigils still black.

Upstairs, I heard Elena pounding on the door to the basement, screaming for us to let her in. I swung my headlamp toward the door—our only way out. There in the lock was the missing key.

Struggling with the bag, I bolted up the stairs and tried to twist the key but it wouldn't move.

"Alex," Aunt Elena screamed, frantic. "Open this door."

"I'm trying," I cried. "But I can't. It's locked." I worked at the key, trying to twist it open. "It won't budge."

A terrible, cold presence wrapped around me from behind. I swung toward the basement. Toward my friends. But my thin beam of light dimmed into nothingness. Mr. Wilkes was a large, black mass, and he grew almost as huge as the room. "You're not going anywhere," he growled.

I needed to think and fast. The tattoo at the base of my skull burned. I grabbed my mom's Nazar Boncuğu amulet, whispered a prayer, then dove down half a flight of stairs for the ghostball at Frank's feet.

The lamp on my head went flying as I collided with the concrete floor and my hip scar screamed in agony. The pain made my vision narrow and swirl with blackness; I thought I'd pass out. But I couldn't. I had to stop Mr. Wilkes. I had to save my friends.

I grabbed the sigiled ghostball and Mr. Wilkes lunged at me. My vision went black and a terrible iciness coated my skin. Mom's amulet grew warm against my chest and it began to radiate a brilliant blue. Then the tattoo at the base of my skull burned, but I ignored it, held up the ghostball, and prayed the sigils would trap Mr. Wilkes inside.

The pressure on my neck tightened, strangling the breath from my throat. Aunt Elena kept pounding on the door, her voice garbled and high-pitched with fear. Mrs. Wilkes screamed from inside my bag. I had to use the ward.

I drew in what little breath I could and hissed it out. "By the light, on this day, I call to Thee to give me Your might. By the power of three, I command Thee into this ball. Lord protect all that surround me. So may it be. So may it be."

Mr. Wilkes let out a great wail. Then everything went silent. My headlamp lay sideways on the floor, its beam illuminating the smashed wall. Frank fell to his knees, coughing, and I heard Jason cry out.

Hannah scrambled over the broken bricks to Jason and wiped the blood from his face.

"Oh, dear. Oh, dear. Oh, dear." Mrs. Wilkes's spirit rose out of my backpack and she spun in circles. "Where is he?"

Very slowly I got to my knees and then stood, the ghostball clutched to my chest. The sigils sizzled with golden light. We'd done it. The ghostball had worked. I had Mr. Wilkes trapped inside.

CHAPTER EIGHTEEN

Aunt Elena had taken Jason and Hannah back home to grab some food and drinks for us. I honestly think they needed a break after what we'd experienced in the Wilkeses' basement. Knowing they were safe at Elena's made me feel a little better. Well enough to take our ghostball trap and Mrs. Wilkes to Lafayette Cemetery No. 1.

Backpack on my lap, I tried to ignore the shape of Mrs. Wilkes's bones, which poked me through the bag. Thankfully she'd settled back into her bones and had been quiet ever since.

Frank kept to the speed limit. I guess he didn't want to get pulled over for a speeding ticket, but I wished he'd go faster. I wanted this over and done with.

"I talked to Harry Graves yesterday. He said the Wilkeses have a family mausoleum and there's a spot we can put Mrs. Wilkes. So, we'll inter her there." Frank kept blotting sweat from his forehead. He and Hannah and Jason had all been tired and wet after they got unfrozen; sort of like they'd been defrosted. Frank had fared the best. He said his tattoos kept away the worst of Mr. Wilkes's evil. Frank kept his eyes on the road; the ghostball with Mr. Wilkes's spirit quivered between us, the sigils flaring gold and silver.

I eyed the ball suspiciously. When I'd played ghostball, the balls didn't move until they were "activated" by the team psychic. The trapped spirit was brought out of some sort of stasis and would then move the ball. I'd never seen one glow and quiver so much. "So, um, Frank. Why is the ball jumping around like that?" I banished the thought of Mr. Wilkes escaping in the car and attacking us.

Frank's gaze flickered to the ball, then back to the road. "It's not an official ghost trap. The government spends millions testing their traps." The ball jumped angrily and Frank gave it a thump. "Which they could be more generous with," he added with some bite. "You boys were ingenious to think of using an inactive ghostball as a trap. I just hope the sigils hold long enough for us to help the old boy cross over or transfer him into a more permanent one."

"And how are we supposed to get a real ghost trap if he doesn't cross over?"

"I still have contacts with my old office. Once I sign you on as my apprentice, I'm sure we can arrange something."

"So you'll take me on?" I asked, a mixture of hope and fear making my voice crack.

Frank clinched his jaw. "Well, I certainly can't have you going off half-cocked and getting in more trouble with spirits, can I? And we can't have government hacks sending you off to the Institute of Psychic Studies." He side-eyed me. "Unless you want to get away from here?"

No way did I want to leave my friends and home. And I definitely didn't want to be sent away for testing like some lab specimen. "That's if Dad even believes I am psychic."

"Oh, he'll come around." Frank's grip tightened on the wheel. "There's no doubt about that."

I wasn't so sure, but if Dad would believe anyone, it'd be a Class A Psychic. Even if Dad thought he was a Class A Criminal.

"Here we are." Frank pulled up and parked in front of the wrought-iron gates of Lafayette Cemetery No. 1.

Frank led the way to Mr. Graves's office, Mrs. Wilson's bones poke—poke—poking me in the ribs through my bag with every step.

Mr. Graves stood waiting for us, leaning against the doorframe, a mass of skeleton keys dangling from his hand. His greasy gray hair fluttered and flapped in the September breeze.

I shivered, but it wasn't from the cold.

Mr. Graves quickly led us to the Wilkeses' family mausoleum, which was unnervingly close to Mom's grave. Mr. Graves rushed us right past her tomb, and I tried not to stare. Maybe when I helped Mrs. Wilkes cross over I would finally visit. After all I'd been through with Mrs. Wilson and Janitor Thomas and Mr. and Mrs. Wilkes, I knew Mom wasn't really gone. True, she wasn't here with me physically, but I had no doubt her spirit had survived. I only wished I had one more chance to hug her goodbye. I supposed that's what almost anyone who's lost someone wants. Another minute. Another hour. Another lifetime.

I shoved down my sadness and followed Frank and Mr. Graves along the foot-worn paths between the tombs and towering oak trees. We stopped at a massive stone mausoleum with the Wilkeses' name inscribed on the marble front. Barring the door were wrought-iron gates, chained closed. Behind those were heavy-looking doors partially filled with names of the dead.

"There'll be plenty of room in there." Mr. Graves flipped through several large keys before finding the one he wanted. He inserted the key in the large lock. With some effort, the key turned and the lock opened. He let the chain fall to the ground and creaked open the ancient-looking metal doors.

He shuffled through his keys again. "It's been a while since I've been in here." He tried one key, then another. "Can't remember which one . . ." Finally, he tried a key that worked and the lock clicked open. "Ah, here we go."

Turning the handle and shoving his full weight against the door, Mr. Graves forced it open. I peered in to a seam of blackness. Hopefully Mrs. Wilkes would go peacefully.

Mr. Graves stepped back, eyeing me and then Frank. "Well, in you go."

"Don't we need to call the police and let them know we've discovered Mrs. Wilkes's remains?" I asked, stalling my inevitable journey into the tomb.

"No time." Frank's words were clipped. "I spoke to the family. They want her put to rest. I'll file a report later and they'll have a small service. But it's important to get her bones into hallowed ground." A rumble sounded in the sky and a splatter of rain hit my face.

"If we want to put Mrs. Wilkes to rest before her husband escapes our little trap here, then we'd better get a move on." Frank lifted the ball, which trembled in his hands. It was almost as if Mr. Wilkes heard us from inside and wasn't happy about what we were fixing to do.

Mr. Graves took a step back. "You use a traditional ghost trap?" he snapped at Frank.

"I don't work for the government anymore, Harry. You know how it is. I can only pull so many strings. And the boys here were smart to think of using this." He shoved the ghostball trap into his own satchel and nodded at the mausoleum door as more droplets fell from the darkening sky. "Let's get on with it."

"For God's sake, be careful," Mr. Graves hissed and took off across the graveyard, back to the safety of his little office.

Frank led the way inside. I was glad to have him here, and relieved that Jason and Hannah had escaped this part of our plan.

The mausoleum was old, well over a hundred years by the looks of it. There were several rows of coffins slid into the wall niches. Some were new, others were rotting. I saw a bit of bone through the rotten space of one coffin and tried to suppress a shudder.

As my eyes adjusted to the dark, musty tomb, a raspy gasp escaped somewhere close to my ear and an icy chill slithered along my arms and spine. Mrs. Wilkes floated past me, pale and translucent. But she didn't look frightened anymore. "That's my sister," she said, pointing to one of the newer coffins. "And there's Harold.

"That was the one nice thing my husband did for me. He let my family be buried here. He said I should be buried next to him." She shivered, then sniffed. "But I'd like to go beside Mamma an' Daddy." She pointed to an open niche toward the top.

I stood there dumbstruck until Frank nudged me. "Get on with it."

"What am I supposed to do?" I felt stupid, but surely there had to be more than simply setting her bones in the wall.

Frank sighed. "Put her bones in the wall and ask her if she sees the light. I'll help if you need it."

The ghostball trap made a weird, strangled moaning sound and Frank clamped his arm down on it hard. "Go on, now. Hurry up before we have to deal with him."

I nodded and cleared my throat. "Mrs. Wilkes. It's time you went to see your family," I said, stumbling over my words. I had no idea if what I was saying was right. "I'm going to place your remains there—" I pointed at the niche beside her mother and father. "Then you can rest."

Mrs. Wilkes nodded, and a look of hope filled her face. "Oh, my."

"Do you see a light?" Could it really be this easy?

Frank started mumbling a prayer that I didn't quite catch.

"I see it." Her mouth opened in awe.

Somehow I knew this was my chance. I placed the bag with Mrs. Wilkes's bones into the niche.

When I looked back at her spirit, Mrs. Wilkes was fading fast in a halo of white light with a smile on her face. "Mamma. Daddy." Her arms outstretched, she took a last step forward and then disappeared.

The room went suddenly dark and quiet except for the pitter-pat of rain falling on the roof overhead.

Frank gave me a thumbs-up through the gloom. "Nice job, Alex. Now let's see about putting Mr. Wilkes to rest before he escapes."

For the first time I thought that maybe being a psychic wasn't such a bad thing. I'd actually helped Mrs. Wilkes escape her tomb in the basement wall. I'd taken her bones and laid her to rest. And I'd helped her cross over. I wondered how many more spirits I might be able to help if I kept at it. I'd definitely need Frank's help and Aunt Elena's guidance, but now I knew I could do it.

That's when I heard the one living voice I didn't want to hear in this place. Dad.

He barged into the mausoleum and I swear his cheeks glowed red even in the dark. "Alex Lenard. You are coming home with me right now. Enough of this nonsense."

My heart sank into my toes. How could I help anybody when Dad didn't even believe in me?

Breathless, Jason, Hannah, and Aunt Elena all piled in behind Dad, making our already cramped space even tighter. I shot Jason a Why'd-you-bring-him? look.

"He was at my house when I ran in for a shirt that wasn't soaked in my own blood," Jason protested, his nose looking really swollen. "What was I supposed to do? It was bring him or don't come."

"Now, Alex," Dad cut in.

Frank stepped between me and Dad, the ghostball trap still clutched tightly in his hands. "Alex's not going anywhere."

"Excuse me?" Dad's cheeks puffed out like some sort of demented blowfish.

"I'm Frank Martinez, a retired Class A Federal Psychic and experienced paranormal investigator. This boy has more psychic power than anyone I've come across in my career. And right now he happens to be in the middle of a job."

"A—a what?" Dad sputtered. "He's no psychic." Dad took a stride around Frank and grabbed my arm. "We're going. Now."

Frank shoved the ghostball trap under one arm and put his free hand on Dad. "Mr. Lenard. Alex isn't finished."

Dad jerked his arm away from Frank, knocking the ghostball from Frank's grasp. The sigils flared gold then went dark.

I saw Frank's lips form the word "no," but I didn't hear a sound. Time seemed to slow and the air in the crypt turned to ice.

Mr. Wilkes's spirit exploded from the ball with a frigid wail.

Dad, Aunt Elena, Jason, and Hannah all fell to their knees, hands covering their ears, their faces filled with terror.

Frank struggled to stand. He mumbled something, probably a ward. But Mr. Wilkes lunged at him, knocking him to the ground. Frank gave a startled cry as the spirit pounced on him, and I could barely make out his words. "Too powerful. Need backup."

Backup? There was no time to go for backup. And who would I even get? Everyone was going to die and there was nothing I could do about it. Why had I ever listened to my aunt and cousin? I should have ignored my new abilities. Ignored Hannah. Ignored the ghosts.

The chill grew stronger and I couldn't ignore the malevolent spirit. Not with everyone I cared about huddled and defenseless and Frank now limp and moaning. At least they were still alive. Mr. Wilkes's huge form raised up, glaring at me.

It was now or never. I may not be a skilled psychic, but if I had the power Frank and Aunt Elena seemed to think they'd seen in me, then I had to use it. If I didn't, we'd all die.

Susan McCauley

Chapter Nineteen

Mr. Wilkes lunged toward me, shoving me hard against the stone wall of the mausoleum. A horrific iciness coated my skin and his hands tightened around my neck. I barely noticed the pain in my tattoo any longer. Pain that somehow now seemed part of my gift.

Invisible hands squeezed my neck. I only knew the one ward-prayer Frank had taught me. I hoped that it, along with Mom's amulet and Aunt Elena's pendant, would be enough to send Mr. Wilkes to the other side.

Struggling to stand, I grabbed on to the amulet and said the prayer of crossing over I'd learned in Frank's book. "No matter what you've done or what you fear, spirit, your place to stay is no longer here. Your life and time is now complete. Move into the light that shines before you, then in time you'll be cleansed."

Mr. Wilkes roared at me, his grip so tight I started to choke. My vision grew dim.

Suddenly a vortex of light and dark opened up behind Mr. Wilkes. And the Nazar Boncuğu around my neck got warm and began to glow. Then I heard a voice from the light.

Mom's voice.

"Alex. The amulet will help you. But you have the power to cross him over. You can do it, son. I'm with you. I'll always be with you." Her voice faded away, and I wasn't afraid anymore. And now I knew I could use these powers, however unwanted, to help the living and the dead.

I raised the amulet before me. "Mr. Wilkes, it's time to cross over. Your time here is done." The Nazar Boncuğu glowed a brilliant blue and I pushed it into the icy black mass that was Mr. Wilkes.

The wind inside the tomb screamed, Mr. Wilkes's wails lost among the torrent. Thunder boomed overhead and my amulet blazed.

The vortex of light and dark opened up wider behind Mr. Wilkes. His dark shape, illuminated by the light, shrank into that of a pale, hunched old man. He was nearly solid. The familiar glare flared in his eyes, but now there was something else there, too. Fear.

He looked from me to the coffins to the swirling vortex behind him. He struggled toward me, his bony arms outstretched, but the vortex pulled him backward.

Mr. Wilkes screamed. He didn't look angry anymore. Just terrified. "Please," he screamed. "Please, Eleanor, forgive me. Forgive me." Tears streamed down his face as he was pulled backward into the swirling vortex of light and dark.

My amulet flashed a blinding blue; there was a final high-pitched wail and the sound of breaking glass. I collapsed to the ground. And all was silent.

It seemed like I'd sat there in the dark for nearly an hour. But maybe it had been only minutes. Eventually, my heart slowed and my raspy gasps returned to normal. Rain pitter-pattered overhead. Frank moaned and there was movement from the others.

I reached for Mom's amulet, but found only my pendant. I rose on unsteady feet and scanned the room.

There, in the spot where Mr. Wilkes had disappeared, lay Mom's amulet. My Nazar Boncuğu. Broken.

With tears in my eyes, I picked up the two halves, cold in my hands.

"Alex." Dad's voice cracked. He crawled toward me in the stormy evening light that shone in through the mausoleum doors. "Your mother's amulet."

My heart twisted into knots. "I know," I mumbled. "It's broken."

Dad slowly climbed to his feet. "No. I saw it glow. I saw white light coming from all around you." He took a huge gulp of air and his voice cracked. "I heard your mother." Tears streamed down his face.

"You heard?" I couldn't believe it. Dad had actually heard something supernatural.

Frank pulled himself up into a sitting position now. "If the power is strong enough," he said, sounding exhausted, "even the Untouched will hear and see some things."

Jason and Hannah and Elena were all on their feet now. Elena seemed calm as usual. Hannah's eyes were bigger than boiled eggs. And Jason. Jason had a huge, freaked-out grin on his face. Right under his big swollen nose.

"That was totally wicked cool, X," he said, and gave me a high five.

I swear, J was the best best friend ever.

"You saved us." Hannah's voice quivered. "All of us. And that nasty Mr. Wilkes is gone."

I wondered where he went. Heaven? Hell? They must exist, even if it wasn't the way I'd imagined.

Dad shook his head. "How is it possible? You're too old to become a psychic."

Frank mumbled something to Dad and weakly led us from the tomb. "Sometimes the supernatural changes the rules on us, Mr. Lenard. And I think the accident brought Alex so close to death that it gave him a gift. Even his mother knew. She made certain he had the protection of her Nazar Boncuğu before she crossed over." He gestured to the broken amulet in my hands. "Your son is the most powerful psychic I've ever encountered."

I might not be a ghostball player anymore, or the most popular kid in school. But what I had now was even more special. I'd lost my mom, but in surviving I had gained a gift. A gift that would allow me to help lonely lost spirits cross over. A gift that would send malevolent spirits wherever they needed to go to atone for their crimes. A gift I was glad I didn't have to give back.

Susan McCauley

Chapter Twenty

The following week, I'd attended a small funeral service for Mrs. Wilkes with my dad and Aunt Elena and the Wilkeses' immediate family. Even Jason and Hannah had been given permission to leave school early for the service.

I'd just walked in our front door from visiting Mom's grave where I'd finished reading The Graveyard Book. I tossed my backpack on the floor by the hall tree, suddenly glad I wasn't like Bod. He'd lost both his parents when he was too young to remember them. At least I had Dad. And I knew my mother. I'd always remember her. I'd always love her.

Raised voices stopped me. I checked my watch: four o'clock. Dad wasn't due home until six.

The voices definitely belonged to a man and a woman. I hoped I didn't have a new ghost problem to deal with—not yet, anyway. Frank was supposed to officially start my apprenticeship on Monday. Then there'd be no more regular school for me; I'd be off to an apprenticeship to learn how to be a professional psychic. I wouldn't miss Billy or David or being badgered to rejoin the team. But I was still a little sad. Oh, well. At least the OPI wasn't going to force me to attend a psychic boarding school out of state. They'd agreed that under my "special circumstance" of becoming psychic after age ten, and having a master Class A Psychic like Frank Martinez around to teach me, that I could stay in New Orleans and learn from the best. And I'd still get to see Hannah and Jason in the afternoons.

A deep-chested chuckle followed by a high-pitched tittering laugh pulled from my thoughts. It was Mrs. Wilson's laugh. Don't tell me she could actually have ghost friends over to visit.

I frowned and went up to my room.

Mrs. Wilson sat sprawled comfortably on my bed, and there, in the corner chair, perched Janitor Thomas.

"Mr. Thomas." I'd been so upset he'd sacrificed himself to save me from Mr. Wilkes, but in all the recent excitement I'd nearly forgotten to ask Frank about helping him.

"Hello, there, Alex." Mr. Thomas smiled, the bullet holes still oozing blood onto his crisp white shirt.

They didn't look so scary anymore, and neither did Mr. Thomas. I ran up and hugged him—or tried to. My arms slid right through him, leaving a slimy chill. I had yet to learn to touch a ghost. So, I shrugged and we all laughed.

"Where did you go?" I asked him and pulled out the journal Frank had given me with the command to write down everything I learned about the other side.

Mr. Thomas scratched his head. "I don't entirely know. It was dark and cold. Somewhere in between, I think."

"In between?" I asked.

Mr. Thomas and Mrs. Wilson shared a knowing look, which sort of irked me, but I didn't say anything. I wanted to understand. So, I wrote it down in my new notebook: in between?

"In between here and there." Mr. Thomas rose to his feet and began to disappear.

"Where are you going?" Alarm lilted my voice.

"Back to school, child." His brilliant white teeth nearly glowed against his dark skin. "Back to school."

"Are you sure?" I asked. "I—er, I mean can I help you cross over?"

"Maybe someday, Alex. But for now, it's back to school. I love it too much to leave." And with that Mr. Thomas faded away.

I turned to Mrs. Wilson, who was now politely seated on the edge of my bed. As much as I didn't want to let her go, being like a surrogate mom and all, I knew she had business on the other side. "And what about you?" I asked with a gulp. "I can help you, Mrs. Wilson?"

"I know you can, Alex. You're a good boy. Such a good boy." She patted my arm, leaving the usual icy feeling on my skin. "And if you'd have found me a year ago, I'd have said yes in a snap." She clicked her translucent fingers together, making a clicking sound.

My chest tightened and I clenched my teeth. Nope. I wouldn't cry. It was my job. My duty to help spirits cross over, and I would help Mrs. Wilson.

Mrs. Wilson reached out toward me, but stopped just shy of touching me. "But not now, Alex. I'm not ready anymore."

"What do you mean?" I sat next to her with a mixture of relief and confusion.

"Well, for years and years I waited for my son to come home. Never mind that he moved away years ago."

I tried to say something to comfort her, but she cut me off. "It's okay. I'm sure he grew up and had a family, which is as it should be."

The sadness in her voice made my heart ache. If only I could give her son back to her. But that was impossible. I could maybe find out where he'd gone, but I couldn't give him back to her. Not any more than she could give my mom back to me.

She patted my leg and I shivered. "I'll see him again one day, Alex. One day, when I'm ready, you can help me cross into the light. And when he arrives, I'll be waiting for him."

"But why not now?" I asked, hoping she would really stay.

"I've got you now." She smiled. "And with all the fuss about your being psychic and all, and your daddy still getting used to the idea, I figure you're going to need me."

An uncertain tinge of happiness spread through my chest. I had Frank and Aunt Elena and Hannah and Jason, but having a ghost on my team would certainly be a benefit. A big smile crept onto my face; I could have hugged Mrs. Wilson if my arms didn't slip through her. Maybe someday I'd be able to touch her like she seemed to be able to touch me. Then the doorbell rang.

"You'd better get that."

I nodded and got to my feet. "Thanks, Mrs. Wilson."

She cocked her head to one side. "For what?"

"For staying."

Hannah and Jason were at the door, both with school backpacks slung over their shoulders.

"X, you're so lucky you don't have to go back to school." Jason pushed past me into the house and headed straight for the kitchen.

Hannah laughed and we followed Jason to the fridge. "The whole school knows what you did with the Wilkeses now. Nobody can believe you're actually psychic," she said in that smug way only Hannah can.

Jason pulled open the refrigerator door. He took out a cold piece of pizza and shoved it in his mouth. "Well, get on wit' it," he mumbled through his mouthful.

Hannah rolled her eyes. "You're totally disgusting when you do that."

Jason chewed a couple times then opened his mouth wide.

"G-ross." Hannah set down her backpack and unzipped it.

Jason kept chewing loudly.

I laughed.

"We brought something for you." Hannah handed me a black box tied with a brilliant blue ribbon. "It's from both of us to help with the start of your new adventure."

She gestured to the box and Jason stopped chewing, waiting for me to open it.

"Er, thanks," I said. "I didn't expect anything." My friends were the best.

"Oh, just open it." Hannah stomped her foot.

I tugged off the blue ribbon and opened the box. There inside, lying on a black velvet bed, was a beautiful new Nazar Boncuğu.

It wasn't Mom's—it was slightly smaller, and the coloring wasn't quite as bright blue. But it was brilliant just the same because it came from two of the people I loved most. My cousin and my best friend.

Susan McCauley

GLOSSARY

Clairaudient: A psychic who can hear or perceive sounds, voices, or noise from the spiritual realm.

Clairscent: A psychic who can smell an odor or fragrance that is not in the physical world, but emanates from a spirit or the spirit world.

Clairsentient: A psychic who gathers information by feeling with the whole body.

Class A Psychics: The strongest psychics belong to this class. They can see, feel, smell, and hear ghosts and other supernatural entities. Class A Psychics make up just under 1 percent of all living humans.

Class B Psychics: The second strongest class of psychics. These psychics can either see and feel or hear and feel ghosts, but not both. Class B Psychics make up about 2 percent of all living humans.

Class C Psychics: The weakest class of psychics. Class C Psychics can feel ghosts at times, but they aren't able to see or hear them with any degree of predictability. Class C Psychics make up slightly more than 1 percent of all living humans.

Electromagnetic field (EMF): A physical field produced by electrically charged objects. Electrical currents and living creatures can affect the EMF; however, if a spirit is present, the EMF may be highly charged.

Electronic voice phenomena (EVP): Sounds found on electronic recordings interpreted as spirit voices. These voices are not audible to the Untouched or lower-class psychics when they are recorded.

EVP listener: A device to record electronic voice phenomena (EVP).

Gauss Master EMF meter: A scientific instrument that detects waves in the electromagnetic field. This instrument helps paranormal investigators detect the presence of spirits without a psychic present.

God's eye ("Ojo de Dios"): A spiritual object that originated in Mexico. It is made by weaving a design out of colorful yarn on a wooden cross.

Ghost: The apparition of a dead person in the physical world; a spirit.

Ghostball: 1. A ball with sigils that keep a poltergeist trapped inside so it will move on its own; 2. A game, like soccer, but played with a ghostball.

Holy water: Water that has been blessed by clergy and protects the user against evil.

King Solomon: Also named Jedidiah; King Solomon was a wealthy and wise king of Israel who reigned circa 970 to 931 BCE.

Malevolent spirit: The soul of a human being who had ill intentions while living. Since spirits retain the same personalities they had while alive, these spirits can be angry, troublesome, and just plain nasty.

Nazar Boncuğu: A brilliant blue eye-shaped amulet, traditional in Turkey, which protects against "the evil eye."

Office of Psychic Investigation (OPI): The federal organization in the United States of America that defends the country and its citizens against paranormal attacks. There are federal, state, and city offices of the OPI.

Paranormal Cybersecurity Squad (PCS): A federal organization that monitors all electronics in the United States to aid in the prevention of paranormal cyber- and electronic attacks.

Paranormal Investigator (PI): Usually an Untouched or someone with little psychic ability who investigates paranormal activity.

Pentacle: A talisman or magical object, typically disk-shaped and inscribed with a pentagram (a five-pointed star). A pentacle can sometimes be found in the Seals of Solomon, which wards against evil spirits.

Poltergeist: A supernatural being of unknown origin responsible for loud noises and throwing objects around.

Pretender: An Untouched (nonpsychic) who so desperately wants to be psychic that they pretend to be one.

Seal of Solomon: The legend of the Seal of Solomon is that the ring was engraved by God and was given to the king directly from heaven. There are forty-four Seals of Solomon, some of which can be used for protection against evil.

Sigil: An inscribed or painted symbol that contains magical power. Often used to keep ghosts and spirits out of homes, offices, schools, etc.

Sixth Pentacle of Mars: A Seal of Solomon that protects its owner against harm and causes an enemy's weapons to turn against him.

Spellguard watch: The safest electronic watch on the planet with sigils inscribed on every gear and battery. The seal on the face glows in the dark. It is the standard-issue watch for every Paranormal Cybersecurity Squad officer.

The Great Unleashing: When American and British spiritualists opened the door from the world of the dead to the world of the living and allowed ghosts and other supernatural beings to roam freely. They were unable to close the door they opened.

The Problem: When ghosts and spirits roam freely in the world of the living due to the Great Unleashing.

Third Pentacle of Jupiter: One of the Seals of Solomon. This seal defends and protects those who encounter spirits.

Town psychic: Local psychics, usually operated by Class B or Class C Psychics, not directly regulated by the OPI. The town psychics take smaller cases that the local or federal OPI offices are too busy to handle.

Untouched: A nonpsychic person. The Untouched make up roughly 96 percent of the entire living population.

Ward: A type of magic or spell intended to deflect harm or evil.

Acknowledgements

First, thank you readers for giving this book life. Your support is truly appreciated.

I must also thank my amazing editor, Deborah Halverson, who has supported and encouraged me through my journey of writing of *Ghost Hunters: Bones in the Wall* (and beyond). Thank you to Dan Janeck for his brilliant copyediting skills. Thanks also to the amazing cover designer Christian Bentulan for his stunning cover work, and to the team at Dragon Realm Press for all that you do to help make my books look amazing and to get them into the hands of readers. Last, but definitely not least, thank you to my fabulous attorney, Charlotte A. Hassett, Esq., for her sound legal counsel and for keeping me grounded when I'm overwhelmed. What an awesome team!

Thanks to my critique partner and friend, James R. Hannibal, for his continued encouragement; to Pat Cuchens, my sweet friend and grammar guru, who catches pretty much all of my typos and grammar snafus, and who lends her emotional support whenever I need it; to the fabulous T.J. Resler, who writes amazing *National Geographic* books for kids and makes writing conferences so much fun. Thank you to my friends at the Horror Writers Association (HWA) and the Society of Children's Book Writers and Illustrators (SCBWI) for supporting and encouraging me and so many writers. And thanks to all of my family and friends who have believed in me and my writing over the years.

Finally, thank you to my mother, Sandy Basso, who reads and gives me feedback on everything I write; I don't know what I would do without you. And, last, but certainly not least, thank you to my husband, Rick, and my son, Alex, who have supported me through the ups and downs of the writing process, have had patience when I had to write despite them wanting me to do something else, and for their endless love and support.

About the Author

Susan McCauley has been intrigued by ghost stories since she was first enchanted and scared witless on Disney's Haunted Mansion ride at the age of three. She now writes works of horror, paranormal, and dark fantasy (with a particular fondness for ghost stories). She lives in Houston, Texas with her husband, son, three crazy cats, and a wide variety of other pets.

To get the latest news, check out www.sbmccauley.com or connect with her on social media.

If you enjoyed this book, please leave a review with your favorite book retailer, on Goodreads, or both—it will be immensely appreciated!

CPSIA information can be obtained
at www.ICGtesting.com
Printed in the USA
LVHW091512250820
664206LV00007B/74/J